Vesper examined her sleeve, which had been torn along much of its length. "That's odd. My jacket's ruined too."

At first, I assumed that she had also been attacked by the ferocious donkey. A closer look showed me that her arm had been slashed and was bleeding copiously.

"I feel like something stung me." Vesper frowned. "It happened just when you fell. I started to pull you loose—"

My handkerchief was gone. I flung off my coat and ripped my shirt to strips, despite the astonished glances from the passersby.

"Dear girl," I cried, trying to improvise a bandage, "you've had a frightful accident."

"No accident," said Vesper. "Somebody tried to stab me."

LLOYD ALEXANDER, a resident of Drexel Hill, Pennsylvania, is the author of *Westmark, The Kestrel, The Beggar Queen,* and The Prydain Chronicles, including *The Book of Three, The Black Cauldron* (a Newbery Honor Book), *The Castle of Llyr, Taran Wanderer,* and *The High King* (winner of the Newbery Medal), all available in Dell Laurel-Leaf editions.

# The
# Illyrian Adventure

LLOYD ALEXANDER

Published by
Dell Publishing Co., Inc.
1 Dag Hammarskjold Plaza
New York, New York 10017

Laurel-Leaf Library ® TM 766734, Dell Publishing Co., Inc.

ISBN: 0-440-94018-4

RL: 7.6

Reprinted by arrangement with E. P. Dutton, a division of New American Library

Printed in the United States of America

March 1987

10 9 8 7 6 5 4 3 2 1

WFH

for my daughter
and for my grandchildren

*The Illyrian Adventure*

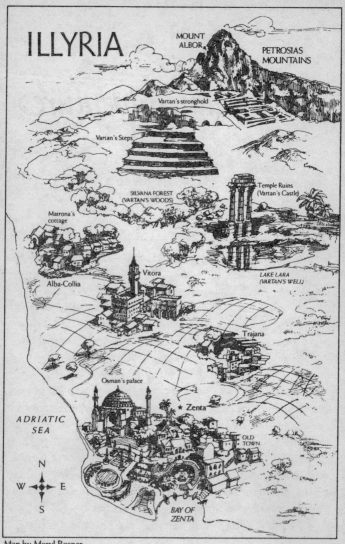

Map by Meryl Rosner

# CHAPTER

## 1

Miss Vesper Holly has the digestive talents of a goat and the mind of a chess master. She is familiar with half a dozen languages and can swear fluently in all of them. She understands the use of a slide rule but prefers doing calculations in her head. She does not hesitate to risk life and limb—mine as well as her own. No doubt she has other qualities as yet undiscovered. I hope not.

But I am getting ahead of my account. I should begin with that day in 1872 when my wife, Mary, and I drove to the Holly estate in Strafford, near Philadelphia. Vesper herself received us in the hallway of the main house. She expected us. What I expected was a pallid little orphan.

What I saw was a girl of sixteen, almost my own height, with sharp green eyes and waist-long hair of an astonishing marmalade hue. She wore a red caftan and purple slippers. She did not appear to require consolation.

"The first thing," said Vesper, "is what shall I call you?

The second thing is lunch." She clapped her hands. "Hop-la! Come along, Moggie."

Vesper directed this order not to us but to an enormous orange cat who scampered after her as she led us into the drawing room. The casement windows had been opened; it was one of those mild March days which Philadelphia, with Quaker thriftiness, doles out sparingly. Vesper settled into an armchair and propped her long legs on a Turkish hassock. Moggie sprang to her lap and curled up there. Vesper noticed that I was looking puzzled by her unusual garment.

"Father sent it from Algiers," she said. "He'd have wanted me to wear it. Why pile on black veils? They don't help. They only make you look like a walking obituary.

"Now, what should it be?" Vesper went on. "Aunt Mary? Yes, I like that." She cupped her chin in her hand and studied me carefully. "Professor? Professor Garrett? No, that won't do."

"Uncle Brinton," I suggested.

"That sounds like something being poured out of a jug," said Vesper. "Father always called you 'Brinnie.' So will I. You're definitely a Brinnie."

Having settled the question, Vesper glanced at the letter I handed to her. I had received it that morning from the law offices of Kenge & Carboy. It notified me that my old friend and traveling companion, Dr. Benjamin Rittenhouse Holly, had died on the Greek island of Mykonos; I had been named executor of his estate and custodian of his personal papers, charged with ordering them for eventual publication.

Further, to our surprise, Mary and I had been appointed guardians of his daughter.

4

"I already know about that," said Vesper. "I'm glad. Father was fond of you, Brinnie. He wouldn't have chosen anyone else."

I told Vesper I was touched and flattered.

"Better than flattery," said Vesper. "He trusted you absolutely. He also knew you were rich enough not to want to line your pockets with my money. And you did save his life once."

Mary blinked at me. "You never said a word about that."

"It's true," said Vesper. "Father wrote me. In Ankara, a pack of bazaar ruffians would have sliced him to pieces if Brinnie hadn't come to the rescue. He told me Brinnie fought like a tiger."

Her father, I reminded Vesper, was known to exaggerate.

"Don't be modest, Brinnie." Vesper grinned at me. "I'm sure you were a wonderful tiger."

Vesper pursued the subject no further, as the housekeeper summoned us to lunch. Vesper attacked her food with an enthusiasm I had witnessed only among the starving nomads of the Sahara. I was still somewhat at a loss for words. Not so with Vesper. Between consuming her meal and feeding tidbits to Moggie, she went on about everything from electromagnetism to a whimsical book by an English clergyman. She was indignant that Mrs. Anthony might face prison for insisting on females' right to vote. She also gave us a few brief details concerning her father's last days. In accordance with his wishes, his remains had been consigned to a blazing pyre on the beach, the ashes scattered to wind and waves.

"That's marvelous," Vesper said. "I'd want exactly the

same. The open sky, the bright flames, the wine-dark sea. Of course, I'd expect the weather to be decent.

"Oh— Brinnie, there's something else," she added. "It's important. We'll talk about that once you've settled in."

"Settled in?" I asked. "Where?"

"Here," said Vesper. "Where better?" She turned to Mary. "There's enough room for the Grand Army of the Potomac. You'll have a whole suite to yourselves. With all the papers to sort out, Brinnie can't rattle back and forth between here and Clifton Heights."

Mary was as much taken aback as I was. Vesper had calmly suggested what amounted to a complete upheaval of our lives. Mary had her garden to tend. And I, since exchanging the hardships of travel for domestic bliss, had taken up the gentle art of beekeeping; further, to occupy my time, I had begun writing a history of the Etruscans. Vesper's proposition, though generous, was impossible.

"Bosh," said Vesper. "Aunt Mary will have acres of garden. I'll send a wagon to fetch your beehives. There's every book you'll need in the library."

"Dear girl," I said, "it's quite out of the question."

Four days later, we moved in with Vesper.

"Brinnie, have you ever read the *Illyriad*?"

Vesper came into the library, where I was in the midst of reconciling the household accounts: one of my duties as guardian-executor. A week had passed since Mary and I had been installed—very comfortably—in the Strafford residence, but I had scarcely begun sorting through Holly's papers. Vesper, most of that morning, had been playing her banjo. Its exuberant, saucy plunking assailed me from the

6

drawing room, distracting my attention from financial details.

With the instrument under her arm, Vesper perched on the edge of the desk. She wore her customary daytime garb: a costume featuring a pair of loose-fitting pantaloons, much like that garment the formidable Mrs. Bloomer once made so popular.

"The *Illyriad*," repeated Vesper, as I looked up a little blankly. "You must have read it."

Yes, of course I had—in the child's version and, later, in its entirety. These days, alas, few know it in either form. This twelfth century epic is Illyria's great classic of literature; indeed the only one produced by that country.

"Brinnie, what do you think of Illyria?"

"I think of it," I replied, "as infrequently as possible."

My knowledge of that pocket-sized kingdom on the eastern seacoast of the Adriatic was, in fact, sketchy. In the twelfth century, a people of Turkish extraction, the Zentans, led by their illustrious King Ahmad, had invaded the country. They were opposed by King Vartan. His gallant but hopeless resistance had turned Vartan into a figure of legend—a mixture of King Arthur, El Cid, Charlemagne, and an unsuccessful George Washington. His heroic deeds had provided the material of the *Illyriad*.

Since those distant days, however, the ethnic Illyrians had been at daggers drawn with their Zentan overlords. The present government still spent most of its time and money putting down Illyrian uprisings. The place, in short, was a tinderbox.

"Father wanted to go there."

"That does not surprise me," I said. "Your father had a great liking for tinderboxes."

"He'd been studying the *Illyriad* before he died. He believed those tales were really true."

"Truly imaginary." I explained to Vesper that Vartan and Ahmad had almost certainly existed, but their deeds, as set forth in the epic, were altogether fantastic.

"Father didn't think so. Remember the part where Vartan captured Ahmad then let him go free? Ahmad was so impressed by Vartan's gallantry, he promised to send him a treasure beyond price. Ahmad went home, but died of his wounds before he could keep his promise."

I recalled the passage. A touching scene, but highly improbable. Monarchs in the real world seldom worry about keeping promises.

"Then," said Vesper, "Ahmad's vizier sent an army of magical warriors against Vartan. They beat the Illyrians, Vartan retreated into a cave, and he's been asleep there ever since."

An army of magical warriors, I replied, was a perfect example of sheer fantasy.

"Magical, yes," Vesper said. "That part's fantasy. But they weren't ordinary warriors. There had to be something unusual about them. Clockwork figures? Mechanical men? Whatever they were, they really existed. Father believed it."

I recalled Holly's theory. He had published it some years ago. It had made him the laughingstock of historians and archeologists. I said I thought he had given it up.

"No," said Vesper. "That's what I wanted to talk to you about."

She handed me a sheaf of letters. "He sent me these. He was onto something. He didn't say exactly what, but it convinced him he'd been right all along."

I scanned the pages. Holly had given few details, but clearly he had something in mind that excited and fascinated him.

"What do you say to that, Brinnie?"

It was, I replied, a pity her father died before proving his theory. It would have been an astonishing and important discovery.

"Yes," Vesper said, "and a good sock in the eye for those idiots who made fun of him."

Regrettably, I said, it was too late. We would never know if he was right or not.

"I'm sure he was." Vesper's eyes fixed on some point visible only to herself. Her lips held a little half smile. I had seen the same look on Holly's face just before he proposed swimming a crocodile-infested river.

"We'll know. I'll find out," said Vesper. "I'm going to Illyria. And, Brinnie, so are you."

I assured her this was impossible. As her guardian, I could not allow her to embark on such a journey, even under my protection.

"Father said you were a genius at organizing an expedition, working out the details—nobody came close to dear old Brinnie."

"That was long ago." I understood how much she wished to clear her father's reputation. But, in view of the difficulties and dangers, legal responsibilities did not permit me to encourage her, nor did common sense.

Three weeks later, I found myself putting the finishing touches to our travel arrangements.

During that time, I purchased and assembled equipment, had it crated and readied for shipment. I reserved staterooms on a steamer from Philadelphia to Naples and a coastal freighter from there to Illyria. I confess to a measure of enjoyment at being, as it were, back in harness. Even so, not a moment passed without misgivings. My knowledge of parental duties was slight—something to do with graham crackers and proper underclothing. But those duties certainly did not include dashing off to a country of furious Illyrians and, probably, bad drinking water. Mary, surprisingly, agreed with Vesper though I pointed out that I was the one who would have to take care of the dear girl.

While I collected maps, made inventories and timetables, Vesper dealt with the language problem. She dug out a mildewed grammar of Zentan, the official language, and one of Illyrian, spoken by the ethnic population. Since Zentan resembled Turkish, which we both knew, and Illyrian had familiar Latin roots, we soon had a working knowledge of both tongues.

Vesper continued to pore over Holly's last letters, hoping for a clue she might have overlooked.

"This place he mentions—Alba-Collia. I can't find it on the map. He wanted to go to some kind of horse festival."

This puzzled me. Holly had never been interested in livestock exhibits. Perhaps he was thinking of buying pack animals.

One obstacle lay ahead of us: the *firman*. This document was an authorization from the highest level of government. In Illyria, nothing could be done without it. A *firman*, I knew, was extremely difficult to obtain. Some petitioners waited for years only, in the end, to be refused.

"Don't worry, Brinnie," said Vesper. "I sent a letter to King Osman."

"What?" I cried. "You wrote directly to the king of Illyria?"

"Why not? He gets letters like everyone else, doesn't he?"

"But—but surely you don't expect an answer."

"Of course not," said Vesper. "I told him he needn't write back. We'd see him as soon as we got there."

# 2

"'But 'tis that miracle and queen of gems,'" exclaimed Vesper.

She leaned over the railing of our coastal freighter, shaded her eyes, and peered at the Bay of Zenta: a half moon of bright blue, the clustering buildings of the port dazzling white in air that was Grecian in its clarity.

"I wonder if Shakespeare ever saw Illyria," she said. "Brinnie, it's marvelous. Or it will be, once we're off this floating coal scuttle."

The freighter had turned out to be the grimiest, most unseaworthy vessel in nautical history, evil-smelling even by local standards. Vesper, nevertheless, had proved an excellent sailor. She gained her sea legs the first day out of Philadelphia, explored our steamer from the top deck to the hold, from stem to stern. She suffered not a moment of seasickness, never missed a meal as an honored passenger at the captain's table. This last leg of our voyage was enough to turn a hardy seaman into a devout landlubber. Vesper merely shrugged it off.

For myself, my misgivings multiplied the closer we drew to Illyria. I put them aside, concentrating on the duties awaiting me in Zenta, the capital. I would have to locate our equipment in one of the warehouses, deal with bills of lading, arrange proper storage, then obtain certificates and several dozen other permits—the smaller the country, the greater the amount of paperwork.

At first, it seemed unlikely that Vesper would get beyond the dockside. She caused a stir the moment we set foot inside the customs shed.

"What are they muttering about?" Vesper indicated the port officials and police constables. "We haven't done anything wrong. We haven't been here long enough."

I reminded her that until quite recently the Illyrian women had been obliged to wear black veils and shapeless robes in public. Vesper's trimly cut pantaloons and short overskirt, her hair flying loose, without the token modesty of a hat, would attract a measure of attention.

"Time they got used to it." Vesper smiled sweetly at the customs guard, who scowled and grumbled about *farenkis*—a word applying to any sort of outlander—but who finally let us pass.

We made our way through the horde of ragged urchins and gawking onlookers. Vesper put two fingers in her mouth and gave an earsplitting whistle.

In addition to shattering my eardrums, her signal brought a rattletrap carriage about the size of a dogcart, which somehow hauled us and our baggage to the hotel:

hardly more than a lodging house with a small restaurant whose menu threatened gastric disaster. I suggested seeking accommodations elsewhere.

"It's fine," said Vesper. "We won't be here long anyway."

She engaged the entire second floor—both rooms—and had the proprietor convert it into a kind of suite. She wished to call immediately on King Osman. I insisted on notifying the American consul and transmitting our formal request for an audience through proper official channels. This I did in the course of the day, as well as attending to other details.

Vesper, nevertheless, sent a note to the palace, announcing our arrival.

"Osman probably knows already," she said. "Word gets around. Still, it's only common courtesy."

Vesper got me up at the crack of dawn the next day. We were, she announced, going to visit the Old Town, the Illyrian quarter of Zenta.

"No use wasting time," she said. "We'll have a look around before we hear from Osman."

The Old Town, the lower part of the city, was extremely picturesque. In Philadelphia, it would have been called a slum. The ethnic Illyrians had no choice about living there. Zentan law barred them from any other part of the city, and forbade them owning more than the smallest property or doing anything but the meanest work.

"Half the population's Illyrian," said Vesper. "That's not fair to them. It's plain wrong. I'll have to talk to Osman about it."

As gently as possible, I told Vesper that the likelihood of seeing the king in person was remote—in fact, nil.

Though it distressed me to dampen her spirits, I explained that a ruler like Osman simply did not receive unknown foreigners.

"Unknown?" said Vesper. "Hardly. I told him all about us."

By then, we had reached the heart of the Old Town: a quarter of poor dwellings, narrow streets, and in the center, a kind of bazaar filled with pot sellers, coppersmiths, hawkers of unidentifiable objects, peddlers bawling their wares, and what seemed to be as many donkeys as people.

Vesper had gone into one of the tiny shops when the trouble started.

I heard what sounded like pistol shots, followed by a terrible racket, and, above the din, voices shouting, "Vartan! Vartan!"

Within moments, a crowd of men and women came running down the street. There were screams and more cries of "Vartan!" Vesper, despite my warning, hurried out of the shop.

The press swirled around us. A number of Zentan police had caught up with the crowd. Swinging their truncheons, the officers waded in, flailing right and left. The Illyrians who stood their ground were clubbed and left lying where they fell.

Vesper was no longer at my side. To my consternation, I saw her in the middle of the street.

"You there!" Vesper pointed at one of the constables. "What's this about?"

The officer gaped, taken aback at being addressed in Zentan by an obvious *farenki*. By way of an answer, he tightened his grip on his cudgel and started for Vesper.

By then, I had reached her. I called out that we were

citizens of the United States of America and the Commonwealth of Pennsylvania. Instead of halting, the officer quickened his approach. No doubt he misunderstood my Zentan.

"This is outrageous," Vesper declared. "These people aren't fighting back. They don't even have weapons."

The middle of a riot was not the moment to discuss the rights and wrongs of it. I seized Vesper and joined the fleeing crowd.

My goal was to escape the confines of the Old Town. At the first chance, I pulled Vesper into a side street. We were no better off; a number of Illyrians had taken the same route.

A flight of ancient stone steps rose ahead of us. I hurried Vesper toward it, hoping it would lead to the Zentan area. Vesper suddenly cried out. Also, at that moment, I felt myself assaulted from the rear. I spun around, expecting a Zentan constable. I came face to face with one of the ever-present donkeys.

What the creature was doing there and how it came upon me so suddenly, I was not inclined to guess. The beast was more annoyed than frightened, resentful at finding its way blocked. Braying at the top of its voice, it attempted to push past me.

I fell back, lost my footing, and went sprawling under the hooves. The creature, unable to move one way or the other, could only tread back and forth, marking time, as it were, on whatever portions of my anatomy became available.

Vesper was more stubborn than any Illyrian donkey. By sheer might and main, she succeeded in shoving the beast aside and dragged me clear.

She hustled me up the steps. We did not slow our pace until safely in the Zentan area.

"Are you all right, Brinnie?"

I was, I replied, as well as could be expected.

"Wait a minute then."

Vesper examined her sleeve, which had been torn along much of its length. "That's odd. My jacket's ruined too."

At first, I assumed that she had also been attacked by the ferocious donkey. A closer look showed me that her arm had been slashed and was bleeding copiously.

"It felt like something stung me." Vesper frowned. "It happened when you fell."

My handkerchief was gone. I flung off my coat and ripped my shirt to strips, despite the astonished glances from the passersby.

"Dear girl," I cried, trying to improvise a bandage, "you've had a frightful accident."

"No accident," said Vesper. "Somebody tried to stab me."

"Don't cluck, Brinnie," said Vesper. "I'll be fine. The medical kit's in the hotel room, that's all I need."

The incident, I said, should be reported as soon as possible to the police.

Vesper snorted. "Those head crackers? They don't inspire much confidence. No, I'll deal with this myself."

She whistled up the Zentan translation of a hansom cab. I had, by then, calmed enough to examine her injury more closely. It was unmistakably a knife wound. Had Vesper not moved to help me, the blade would have plunged into her ribs.

"Who'd want to kill me?" said Vesper as we rattled along toward the hotel. "And why?"

I confessed I had no idea. I could imagine no reason at all for such an attack.

"No reason is what bothers me," said Vesper. "There must be a reason. Only we don't know what it is. But somebody had a very good reason. I'll have to think about it."

Once in the privacy of our suite, I hurried to fetch the medical kit. The wound, I was relieved to see, was not as serious as I feared. Vesper was in no way upset by it. She had already turned her mind to another question.

"Why were they shouting 'Vartan'? For the police, it was a red rag to a bull. What riled them so much?"

I had no answer. The whole deplorable business only demonstrated that the country was hardly safe for Illyrians, let alone travelers. While Philadelphia has its shortcomings, riots and assault do not figure prominently in the social scene.

Just then our landlord appeared at the door.

"*Hahnoom!*" he cried—the first time the fellow had used this title of respect. "*Hahnoom,* this is for you."

With much bowing and scraping, he presented a large envelope sealed with red wax. He was fairly jiggling with curiosity, hoping Vesper would examine the contents then and there. She thanked him and waved him away.

"No wonder he was polite," Vesper said. She tore open the envelope and glanced at the letterhead. "It's from the palace. Here, Brinnie, see for yourself."

I expected one of two things: a denial of our *firman,* or at best, some official formality sent by a minor functionary.

It was neither.

Written in excellent English, it granted us a personal audience with His Sublime Majesty, Osman, King of Illyria. There was a postscript penned by the king himself.

> *It will be a pleasure to greet the charming daughter of an illustrious father.*

Vesper grinned all over her face. "I don't like to say I told you so, Brinnie. So I won't. Put it this way: I knew Osman would be delighted to see us."

The following afternoon, adding to the reflected glory of our landlord, a royal carriage pulled up in front of the hotel. In the wake of further bowings and scrapings from the entire hotel staff, it bore us to the palace.

I use the word *palace*, but it was more like a city in itself: parks, fountains, gardens, a Turkish-style *harim*—occupied only by female relatives, for the king was still a bachelor—and a golden-domed central building.

Vesper would have admired its splendors at length, but we had no opportunity, being promptly taken in tow by relays of functionaries, each higher in rank.

At last, we were handed over to a gaunt, hawk-faced individual in a long-skirted black frock coat: Ergon Pasha.

This gentleman was no less a personage than the grand vizier. As chief minister, he occupied the highest office of state next to the king himself. After greeting us with formal courtesy, he left us to cool our heels in an antechamber twice the size of our entire hotel suite.

"I've seen happier undertakers," Vesper said. "I don't think we filled his day with joy."

She broke off at the arrival of a chamberlain wearing a *tarboosh* as tall as a stovepipe, billowing pantaloons, and a gorgeously braided jacket. I expected him to lead us to a hall of state or audience chamber. Instead, he ushered us to one of the king's private apartments: a cool, airy room with a little fountain sparkling at one end.

Ergon Pasha was already there, standing with his hands behind his back and a sour look on his face. King Osman reclined on a divan. Unlike his vizier, he seemed genuinely pleased to see us.

The ruler of Illyria was quite young; a neatly trimmed, dark mustache set off his pale and very handsome features. He did not wear traditional Zentan costume but an excellently tailored lounging suit. He acknowledged my bow with an informal nod. Vesper stepped toward him, not to curtsy but to shake hands; Osman, however, brought her fingertips to his lips—a gesture a Philadelphian would consider a little too familiar. Vesper seemed to enjoy it.

"My dear Miss Holly and Professor Garrett." The king chose to speak in English, as a courtesy to us. "I have met the renowned Dr. Holly only through his publications, but was impressed by him as I am now charmed by his daughter. I trust your stay in my country is proving interesting and pleasant."

"Interesting, yes," replied Vesper. "Pleasant? Well, for one thing, Brinnie nearly got squashed by a donkey in the Old Town. There was a riot going on at the time."

"A small disturbance, Your Majesty," put in Ergon Pasha.

"Indeed?" said Osman. "I was not informed."

"A minor matter. The police dealt with it efficiently. I regret that our distinguished visitors chose that moment to observe the Illyrian quarter." Ergon Pasha tried to look apologetic.

"And something else," Vesper went on. "Not pleasant but very interesting. Somebody tried to kill me."

"Dear Miss Holly, this is most alarming." Osman turned to his vizier. "How can this be? I had assumed—" He broke off and spoke rapidly in Zentan.

"You had us watched?" asked Vesper.

Osman turned to her, embarrassed. Obviously, he had not realized we understood the language. "Your well-being occupied a foremost position in my thoughts. I wished only to provide—what is the term?—a guardian angel."

He frowned at Ergon Pasha. "How could this happen? You assured me our guests would be kept from harm."

"Circumstances made it impossible, Majesty," Ergon Pasha answered smoothly. "The complaint will be thoroughly investigated. This regrettable incident, Majesty, is further proof of the need for strongest measures against these ethnic troublemakers."

Ergon Pasha might have looked like a mortician, but he had not risen to the rank of vizier for nothing. He had, I realized, not only sidestepped his monarch's criticism but also turned it to advantage.

"These rebellions must be stamped out once and for all," Ergon Pasha went on, "without delay, as soon as a punitive force can be raised. As Your Majesty has so wisely agreed."

"Wisely, perhaps," Osman said, "but not willingly."

"You're sending troops against your own people?" put in Vesper.

"Against Illyrians," the vizier corrected.

"This turmoil cannot be allowed to continue," said Osman. "We must have peace. It is vital to my kingdom."

"So you'll crack down on half the population?" Vesper said. "What's peaceful about that?"

"The Illyrians stand in the way of progress," replied Osman. "We desperately need the development of our natural resources, the construction of railroads, of schools and hospitals.

"My vizier has urged me to entrust such projects to the

hands of outsiders, to grant concessions to foreign interests. This I absolutely refuse. Foreign concessions would not enrich us; they would drain us. We would have no control over our own destiny. If we are to keep our independence, we must carry out these projects ourselves."

"What's stopping you?" asked Vesper.

"We cannot," said Osman. "Not while these rebels constantly harass us and destroy all our efforts. They attack our work parties; they tear down what we try to build. They demand what they consider their rights."

"If you ask me," said Vesper, "the answer's obvious."

"His Majesty does not need instruction in government," said Ergon Pasha.

Osman raised his hand. "I shall be interested in Miss Holly's views."

"It's simple," said Vesper. "Give your Illyrians what they want. Why shouldn't they have the same rights as your Zentans? It's their country, too, isn't it? I'd call that plain, ordinary justice."

"Justice?" replied Osman. "You do not understand our Zentan spirit. Here, the king *gives* justice. He does not allow it to be forced from him."

Vesper had struck a nerve with Osman. His face burned —with pride or anger. I hesitated to guess.

"I speak in the name of all my ancestors," Osman declared. "Not one, from the time of King Ahmad himself, has given way to threats. Honor is as important as justice. Generosity, grace—these are gifts a king bestows of his own will. They can only be granted, never demanded. Such is our Zentan code of honor. I follow it, as I follow in the footsteps of King Ahmad. I will not betray his blood that runs in my veins."

"As I remember the *Illyriad*," Vesper said, "after he captured Ahmad, Vartan generously let him go free."

"You prove my point, my dear Miss Holly," replied Osman. "I am happy that you know our literature, but I remind you, Ahmad refused to beg for mercy. He disdained to offer a ransom to save his life. Nor did Vartan bow to threats. He released Ahmad willingly. He was truly a noble enemy, which cannot be said for Vartan today."

"Today?" asked Vesper. "He's been dead for centuries."

"On the contrary," said Osman. "Vartan is alive."

"Alive? He'd be seven hundred years old." Vesper gave the king a slantwise look. "Don't mind me saying so, but that's hard to swallow."

"I am speaking figuratively," said Osman. "The real Vartan is long in his tomb, wherever that may be. As for the legendary Vartan, the *Illyriad* tells that he found refuge in the Petrosias Mountains. There, he fell into a deep sleep and has been slumbering in his cave ever since. But these Illyrians are like children, with all their superstitions and folklore. They devoutly believe he will return."

"When his people need him, he'll come back and save them," said Vesper. "Like King Arthur. Or Charlemagne and Barbarossa."

"Those worthies have stayed sleeping," replied Osman. "Vartan has returned many times. What I mean, Miss Holly, is that any hothead who stirs up the Illyrians against us is looked on as Vartan himself. The name alone is a rallying cry."

"Brinnie and I heard people shouting 'Vartan' in the Old Town. Was he there?"

"I doubt it," said Osman. "That was merely an excuse to make trouble. Our police have yet to learn his real identity, but they assure me he would hardly dare to venture this far south. We have been plagued with a number of so-called Vartans over the years. This newest one is the most dangerous."

"Why should one Vartan be any different from another?"

"He is the most dangerous because he has been the most successful," replied Osman. "He has rallied the peasantry, persuaded them to burn their crops rather than turn them over to their Zentan landlords. He has inspired gangs of brigands to attack our military posts, to steal weapons. He plans no less than a full-scale rebellion against us.

"You understand, Miss Holly, the urgent need for us to move against him and all his followers with utmost severity. The cost, I fear, will be high in money, which my country can ill afford, and in Zentan lives."

"Illyrian lives don't count?"

"They have brought it on themselves," Osman said. "Rebellion cannot go unpunished." He smiled bitterly. "I have often wished for that magical army which our *Illyriad* describes. Alas, I must sacrifice real warriors of flesh and blood, and deal with facts, not fairy tales."

"My father didn't believe that army was a fairy tale."

"As your letter to me suggested. An intriguing notion, Miss Holly. What evidence have you to prove it more than a legend?"

"None," said Vesper. "We came here to find it."

"Your confidence is admirable," said Osman. "How do you propose to do so?"

"I don't know yet," Vesper admitted. "My father mentioned a place called Alba-Collia. We'll start there."

"I am not familiar with it," said Osman.

"I believe it is in the north, Your Majesty," put in Ergon Pasha. "A village in the foothills of the Petrosias. It would be in the Vitora military district."

"Quite so." Osman nodded. "Yes, I recall now there were some disturbances in the region. It is a very backward, superstitious area, and in no way a peaceful one. It would be most unwise for Miss Holly to venture into it."

At this, I broke in to say that we appreciated the dangers of the situation and quite understood why our request for a *firman* must be denied.

"Miss Holly is a courageous young woman," said Osman. "I deplore the risk, but if she wishes to take it, how can I deny her? The *firman* is granted."

Vesper gave me an enormous wink as Osman ordered his vizier to have the document issued.

"I must remind Your Majesty," said Ergon Pasha, "the *firman* requires endorsements and countersignatures from several department heads. The procedure is lengthy."

"We needn't wait," said Vesper, after thanking Osman. "We can leave for Alba-Collia right away. Why lose time? You can send the *firman* to us."

"As you wish," said Osman. "My vizier will make sure it reaches you promptly. I only ask that you communicate with me frequently, for I shall be eager to know of your discoveries. Whatever else you may need, whatever favor, you have my word I shall grant it.

"Perhaps I may assist you further," Osman added. "I have allowed a distinguished scholar to examine and catalog our ancient archives. He is at work in the palace now. Dr. Desmond Helvitius. Do you know him, Professor Garrett?"

I did not recognize the name but answered that I was always eager to meet a colleague.

"So you shall." Osman ordered his vizier to have Dr. Helvitius summoned, then addressed himself again to Vesper.

"Dr. Helvitius is studying our early history, with a view to writing a book on the subject. His research may have uncovered information helpful to you.

"It is unusual for my small country to attract scholarly interest, and I am grateful for it. You see, Miss Holly, I am concerned with our culture as well as with our present difficulties. In time, I hope to build a museum and library. The efforts of Dr. Helvitius will be invaluable."

Osman continued on that topic. I had the impression he preferred it to the unhappy and expensive task of stamping out rebellious ethnics. Vesper offered some suggestions, and the king appeared quite taken with them. Their conversation was interrupted by the arrival of refreshment trays and Dr. Helvitius.

Garbed in heavy tweed knickers and a shooting jacket, he was a large, looming sort, who looked as if he spent more time outdoors than poring over manuscripts. His great shock of white hair added an air of benevolence and good nature. He seemed altogether at ease with Osman and on the best of terms with Ergon Pasha.

"Your father is known to me," Dr. Helvitius told Vesper, "but by reputation only. I never had the pleasure of

28

meeting him. I gather that you share his interest in Illyrian folklore."

Osman explained the purpose of our visit and asked if Dr. Helvitius could shed any light on Holly's theory.

"I have studied the *Illyriad* very closely in connection with my own research." Helvitius spoke with the faintest shadow of an accent I could not identify. "There is no question. The epic does reflect many historical events. I have found proof in His Majesty's archives, which are as complete as any I have seen."

"You are, sir, an archivist? A historian?" I asked. "May I inquire as to the nature of your specialty?"

"I have many specialties." Helvitius smiled with becoming academic modesty. "Geology, botany, chemistry among others. At the moment, I find the study of Illyrian manuscripts especially stimulating."

"You said you found proof," put in Vesper. "That's what I'd like to know about."

"Proof there is," replied Helvitius, "to convince me that this so-called magical army is pure invention, no more than a marvelous literary fancy. Had there been any real basis in actual history, the documents would have made some reference to it."

"I'd like to see those documents for myself," said Vesper.

"I assume, doctor," Osman said to Helvitius, "that would not interfere with your own work?"

"Not at all." Helvitius inclined his head toward Vesper. "But I assure you, Miss Holly, your magical army is sheer folkish fantasy. Nothing even remotely resembling it ever existed. Of that, I am entirely satisfied."

"You are," said Vesper. "I'm not."

It was agreed that Vesper would return the next day. Helvitius would have all the documents prepared for her scrutiny. While Vesper was at the palace, I would see to having our equipment sent to Vitora, the administrative center nearest Alba-Collia. Colonel Zalik, the local commander, would be notified of our arrival.

"Because, Brinnie," Vesper declared, "we'll go there no matter what the archives show."

Osman now indicated our audience was over. "I have duties less agreeable than conversing with Miss Holly."

With another royal hand-kiss, he reminded Vesper of his promise to help in every way, then added, "Dear Miss Holly, if only it were possible to settle this strife as you suggested; if only I had the means or some basis allowing me to grant an honorable peace. This is my personal wish. As king, I have no choice. I must pursue our campaign against these rebels with vigor, and with deepest regret."

We were escorted to our carriage. "Osman's not a bad fellow," remarked Vesper, as we rode back to our hotel. "He really doesn't enjoy fighting. That's happy news for the Illyrians—the ones who survive."

Next morning, while Vesper rooted among the palace archives, I went to the portside storage warehouse to have our equipment recrated, to make out labels for delivery to Vitora, and to complete the rest of the paperwork. The inspectors and other officials took no pains to conceal their opinion. A *farenki,* or anyone who chose to venture into the Illyrian backlands, was certifiably a lunatic. By then, I had come to share that view.

I was glad, at last, to return to the relative comfort of our lodgings. I had scarcely sat down when Vesper hurried into the room.

"Brinnie, I found something," she began. "Two things, in fact. One of them is Nilo."

# 5

"What, for heaven's sake, is a nilo?" I asked.

"Not what," said Vesper. "Who."

She beckoned to a figure standing in the doorway. "Come in. It's all right. Brinnie's a tiger, but he won't bite you."

The object of Vesper's invitation sidled into the room. He was a gangling, large-framed fellow, his oversized feet encased in scuffed leather boots, one of those Illyrian pill-box caps on the back of his head, his hair tumbling into his eyes. His gait was something between a slouch and a skulk. He halted in front of me and made a disjointed sort of bow.

"I found him in front of the hotel," said Vesper.

"You should have left him there," I said. "Dear girl, why ever did you bring him here?"

"He needs work, Brinnie. He wants to be our *dragoman*. He can drive, cook, do odd jobs. So I hired him."

I replied that she had best unhire him. It was out of the question to employ a total stranger, let alone one picked up like a stray cat.

*"Effendi,"* Nilo ventured to put in, bobbing his head up and down, "stray cat, truest companion. That is an old Illyrian proverb."

"I forgot to tell you," Vesper said. "He knows English."

Nilo grinned sheepishly. I suppose I did likewise.

"He speaks Illyrian and Zentan," Vesper went on. "Best yet, he was born up north. Near Alba-Collia itself. He knows the whole countryside around there, Brinnie. How's that for luck? He's exactly what we need."

What I needed was a little more confidence in the fellow. This Nilo struck me as a feckless specimen. Yet, if he did indeed know the locality, he might be of use. With some reluctance, I agreed he could work for us. I emphasized the word *work*.

Nilo bowed and made grateful Illyrian gestures. "Now I shall take the horses and carriage to a stable for the night, and stay there to watch over them."

There was, I replied, one difficulty. We had neither horses nor carriage.

"We do now," said Vesper. "I didn't see Osman, but he left orders for that chief undertaker of his to give us a royal coach and pair. That saves us having to find our own, which means we can leave first thing in the morning."

Osman's generosity had relieved me of an added chore, for which I was thankful. Nilo, assuring me he was an excellent driver with a deep understanding of horses, ambled off to attend to his duties. Vesper flung herself into a chair.

"I found something fascinating in the archives," she said.

Here, my interest roused. Had she actually turned up some documentary proof of her father's theory?

Vesper shook her head. "What I found was a gap. Plain as a missing tooth. That's interesting, Brinnie. Very curious. The palace records go back centuries: royal orders, letters, every kind of detail. Except for the year when the magical army would have been sent against Vartan."

I reminded Vesper that Dr. Helvitius had said as much.

"No, he didn't. He told us he'd never seen such complete archives."

How then, I asked, did Helvitius explain it?

"All he said was there'd never been any documents for that year. I don't believe him."

A respected scholar, an academic, I replied, would certainly not tell an untruth.

"Maybe. Maybe not," said Vesper. "All I know is that there are plenty of records before, and plenty of records after. Nothing in between. I think somebody took them. Who? When?"

As for when, I answered, they could have been removed any time within the past half-dozen centuries. Or merely lost. Or thrown out by accident. Such things often happened. As for why, that would be impossible to guess. One thing we could be sure of: Neither Dr. Helvitius nor anyone in the palace would deliberately get rid of priceless historical documents.

"I suppose not." Vesper chewed on a thumbnail. "Unless there was a good reason. I can't imagine what. It puzzles me, Brinnie. Well, so much for the archives. They're no help. We'll have to scratch for ourselves. And I mean to keep scratching till I find what we're looking for."

Early next morning, Vesper pounded on my door, urging me to hurry. She goaded me downstairs and into the street. In front of the hotel, Nilo perched on top of a vehicle that looked like a huge packing crate slung between iron-bound wheels. It promised all the comfort of an oxcart.

"This isn't from the palace," explained Vesper. "Nilo sold that one."

"Sold it?" I burst out. "Yes, I'm sure he did—and pocketed the money."

"No, no, *effendi*. I traded it." Nilo spread his hands to fend me off, for I would have collared the wretch then and there. "I kept the horses; they were very fine. But the fancy carriage—*effendi*, believe me, it would fall apart in two days. Less, even. The axle was already half-broken. Very dangerous."

"It was clever of Nilo to see that." Vesper beamed at him. "We might have broken our necks. You should thank him."

As I climbed into that horse-drawn torture chamber, my feelings were not those of gratitude. Later, as we lumbered our way out of the city into the countryside, I admitted that Nilo had acted wisely. We lurched along rutted roads that would have ripped the underpinnings from a less sturdy vehicle. Our bones were rattled by potholes deep as volcano craters. I calculated one bruise per half mile and estimated that by the time we reached Alba-Collia, we would have turned entirely black and blue.

The following days, as we jolted northward past little

35

patchwork quilts of tenant farms, it grew apparent that we had come into a different sort of country.

No doubt the region included a Zentan population, but the look and atmosphere were ethnic Illyrian: the women handsome, bold in their glances, dressed in bright over-skirts; the young men, mostly big, lanky fellows, wearing knee-length vests and embroidered pillbox hats; the old-sters sporting enormous handlebar mustaches.

The Illyrians, by and large, seemed good-natured and spirited and tended to laugh uproariously at their own obscure jokes. I also perceived an underlying edginess. They glowered and muttered among themselves in smouldering surliness whenever a detachment of Zentan troops passed through—not an infrequent occurrence.

As for Nilo, he was never there when he could have been useful and always there when we had no need of him. Otherwise, he mainly spent his time lounging about with the locals.

In Trajana, a village where we stopped to have our horses reshod, Nilo struck up an acquaintance with a big, hard-bitten Illyrian who looked as trustworthy as a highway robber. A scruffy beard covered half his face; the other half was weathered almost black. He was tall, broad-shouldered, and alarmingly muscular. His eyes, deep-set, burned with what could have been some intense, inner fire or simply a bad disposition. A clean shirt would not have harmed him.

Vesper and I chanced upon this individual sitting with Nilo at a rickety table in the *kaffenion-tavierna,* a kind of public house found in even the smallest hamlet.

"I present to you Milan." Nilo bobbed his head and waved an introduction. Milan only muttered and stared us up and down.

"And Silvia." Nilo indicated Milan's companion, an attractive, dark-haired young woman who looked too intelligent to have any dealings with a desperado like Milan.

I was not keen on pursuing the acquaintanceship. Nilo, in my opinion, had fallen into dubious company. But Vesper insisted on sitting down with them and treating them to coffee and honey pastries. Within moments, the dear girl was happily chatting away as if she and Silvia had been childhood friends.

Vesper, indeed, had become more Illyrian than Philadelphian. During our journey, she had acquired the local garb: an embroidered vest, a gaudy kerchief, a pair of threadbare trousers. She looked half-brigand, half-gypsy. I hoped the effect would not be permanent.

After a time, Milan and Silvia left the *kaffenion*. Nilo tagged along with them. He reappeared eventually to announce that the blacksmith had run into some sort of difficulty. By then, it was too late in the day to set out again.

"But I have arranged everything," Nilo assured us. "The *hahnoom* and you, *effendi*, will have rooms above the *kaffenion*. I shall be comfortable in the stable. We have a proverb, *effendi*: To a tired head, straw is as soft as goose down."

If that were true, Illyrian geese must resemble porcupines, for I tossed and turned on my mattress that night. Vesper had taken the delay in good part. To me, it was the latest in a series of mishaps. I had lost count how many times our *dragoman* had followed a wrong road or taken a shortcut leading us to the middle of nowhere.

Our journey, in consequence, was far longer than I had reckoned. At the end of it, I feared, there was every likelihood that the dear child would discover nothing at all.

It also occurred to me that if Osman launched his troops against Vartan in the near future, Vesper and I might well be caught in a hornet's nest.

With these disturbing thoughts in mind, I finally drifted into a doze. A vague sense of some presence roused me. I sat up in bed.

I had only a moment to become aware of a looming shadow. Then a hand was clapped over my mouth.

I tore free of the stifling grasp and rolled out of bed, shouting for help in Illyrian, Zentan, and English. My assailant tried to slip away, but I seized him and tumbled him to the ground.

The door burst open. Vesper, in her night robe, held up a guttering candle.

"Brinnie, what's happened?" she cried. "Why are you choking poor Nilo?"

Nilo indeed it was. Heart still pounding, I called out that the fellow had gone mad and tried to attack me.

"*Effendi*, please, you do not understand. I tried only to warn you." Nilo picked himself up from the floor and scurried to Vesper. "*Hahnoom*, quick! No noise. We must leave here. I have the carriage ready. Dress and pack now."

He turned to me. "Please, *effendi*, hurry. There is a—a small trouble. It is wiser if we do not stay."

A band of rebels, he explained, had been sighted near the village, and Zentan troops were going after them.

"Whether they catch them or not, the Zentans will come back. They will search and question everyone, to learn if the rebels have comrades here. Perhaps they do, perhaps they do not. No matter, some of us will be arrested. Some of us—" Nilo shook his head. "Trust me, *hahnoom*. It is better for us to go. You yourself are in no danger. But with Zentans, who knows? A little caution is good. We have an old proverb: When the dove flies into the myrtle bush, the hungry hawk tightens his belt."

At that moment, there was a commotion in the street below. Some of the villagers had come out of their houses, yelling, flinging curses and insults at a detachment of about a dozen Zentan cavalry galloping by. In reply, a couple of the troopers fired their pistols at random. One of the reckless shots shattered a pane of the window from which I had been observing.

"Come on, Brinnie. Do as Nilo says."

I agreed that he had made a persuasive argument in favor of a hasty departure. We threw our clothing into our bags and hurried down to the stable. Nilo bundled us into the coach.

"We shall not follow the same road as the soldiers," he said, slapping the reins. "I know another way. It is a good shortcut."

He set off as fast as our ungainly vehicle could carry us. The moon was high, shining brilliant white over the countryside. It should have given him light enough to avoid the worst of the ruts and ridges. Nilo managed to jolt us into every one of them. We had covered no great distance when he pulled up and suddenly halted.

Vesper had been drowsing. Nothing kept the dear girl from sleeping when and where she chose. The abrupt stop roused her. "What's wrong, Nilo?"

"Zentans, *bahnoom*," he groaned. "I think they have taken the same shortcut."

Vesper was out of the coach before I could hold her. I followed, fuming at Nilo for this latest piece of idiocy. The incompetent lout had driven us into the very clutches he promised to avoid.

Vesper had seized the reins and, with Nilo's help, tried to turn the horses around. I joined them, but all our efforts were useless. The cavalrymen had, meantime, sighted us and spurred their mounts in our direction.

Four or five of the troopers were upon us within moments, springing from their saddles, pistols drawn. Two collared Nilo and flung him roughly against the side of the coach.

The poor fellow was terrified, babbling pitifully, begging for mercy. The Zentans ripped away his jacket, turned out his pockets, and searched him from head to toe. They found nothing, which seemed to disappoint and anger them. One of the troopers leveled his pistol.

Vesper darted forward instantly. She gave the Zentan a sharp kick in the shins. While he yelped and danced on one leg, his comrade tried to seize Vesper's arms, for the dear girl had begun flailing away at him with both her fists.

Here, I judged it essential for calmness to prevail in what could become a difficult situation. Taking out our travel documents, I hurried to step up and explain matters, at the same time pulling Vesper away from the troopers.

"Let him be," Vesper ordered the Zentans. "He's our *dragoman.*"

The trooper spat. "An Illyrian pig."

"Talk about pigs—" Vesper began.

"*Hahnoom,* say no more," pleaded Nilo.

"I haven't started," replied Vesper.

Fortunately, just then, one of the troopers came back with our papers. His attitude was more respectful than it had been. He went so far as to click his heels and salute as he reported that his officer was satisfied and impressed by our acquaintance with King Osman.

"But this is an extremely dangerous area," he added. "We have already taken a band of these Illyrian brigands. Who knows how many more are hiding in these parts? My captain wishes to escort you part of the way to Alba-Collia."

I told him we would be glad for the protection. The Zentan returned to his comrades. Nilo, relieved, mopped his face and buttoned his torn jacket.

"*Hahnoom,* thank you," he murmured. Hesitant, he added, "I think—with permission—I should call you '*Graciva Lincilla.*' In our language, pretty tiger cub."

Vesper smiled at him. "I'd like that."

The lout stood there gawking and grinning until I had to nudge him into the carriage. We set off again, the Zentan troopers leading.

Delighted though I was to have them with us, I remarked to Vesper that they did not appear well disciplined or very smartly turned out.

"Their captain's no better," observed Vesper, glancing at the officer who wore his peaked cap cocked raffishly over half his face. "I think he put on someone else's uniform by mistake. It's a couple sizes too small."

The Zentan troopers whooped and hallooed as they

drove along the string of horses they had captured. When we halted to rest, they slouched about, congratulating each other on their achievement and taking no precautions whatever against a possible ambush by lurking Illyrians.

They stayed with us the next day and night. We slept in the carriage, uncomfortably but safely. The following dawn, one of their scouts reported seeing Illyrians in the woodlands. Forgetting their escort duties, they all went galloping off, whooping happily, leaving us to our own devices.

By then, we were close to Vitora. Nilo assured us we would have no further trouble. Soon after, he ran the carriage into a ditch. It required all our efforts and much of the afternoon to get it out.

What with Nilo's shortcuts, the Zentan cavalry, and the state of the roads, our journey, which I had calculated would be four days at most, took longer than a week. Midmorning of our last day, we finally reached Vitora, a drab little town. As the administrative center for the region, it was dominated by the Zentan presence. The largest buildings were the field constabulary barracks, the military headquarters, and the jail.

Leaving Nilo guarding our coach and baggage, we reported as instructed to Colonel Zalik, the local *bimbashi.* Commander of the military district, he was also head of the constabulary and first magistrate.

"Dogcatcher, too, I shouldn't wonder," muttered Vesper.

This Colonel Zalik turned out to be a personage of weight, not only administratively but also in the corporeal sense. His massive chest strained the buttons of his tunic. His head had been shaved to the scalp, making it debatable where his face began and ended.

As we introduced ourselves, the *bimbashi* made a vague attempt to get up from his chair, and an even vaguer attempt at a bow.

"Your arrival, *hahnoom*, takes me by surprise. We are not used to visitors. You, indeed, are the first." Zalik settled back to eye Vesper's costume with interest if not with approval. "How may I be of service?"

"We'd like to pick up our *firman* and our equipment," Vesper said. "They both should have come by now."

"*Hahnoom*," Zalik answered, frowning, "you have me at a disadvantage. I understand nothing of this."

"It's all been arranged," Vesper said. "You must have had a message from the palace."

"I have received no instructions whatever." Zalik shook his head. "Until I do—forgive me, *hahnoom*, but I cannot permit you to continue."

"What do you mean, can't permit us?" retorted Vesper. "We've already been permitted."

"Without authorization, without an acceptable document, my duty compels me. No explorations, no expeditions can be allowed. Such are the regulations. As a humble servant of our king, I must follow them."

"I'll send King Osman a letter. Right now," Vesper declared. "He'll straighten this out."

"It will be my pleasure to assist you in any way I can, within the limits of the law." Colonel Zalik offered Vesper a sheet of paper and a pen. While she wrote a message to Osman, the *bimbashi* also jotted some notes. He clapped his hands to summon his orderly, giving over Vesper's message and his own memorandum with instructions to dispatch them instantly by the fastest rider.

"Regarding your equipment," Zalik said. "I can inform you that nothing of such nature has arrived. When it does, I shall be happy to advise you."

"Until then," said Vesper, "I expect your regulations will let us go where we please. We do have travel permits."

"Legally, *hahnoom,* you are free to go where you wish. I repeat, legally. However, I would fail in my duty if I did not warn you against doing so.

"There has been an increase in rebel activity, brigandage, banditry. Most recently, I am informed, one of my cavalry units was ambushed and attacked, horses and weapons stolen, my men stripped and tied to trees. Had a loyal Zentan not chanced by, they would be there still. I should not wish a similar fate upon you, *hahnoom.*"

At that, Zalik dismissed us with added apologies and regrets. Neither did much to satisfy Vesper.

We found Nilo in the street, sitting forlornly on our pile of luggage.

Vesper glanced around. "Where's our carriage?"

"The police have just come and taken it away." Nilo spread his hands and shrugged. "What could I do? One *dragoman* against Zentan officers? *Lincilla,* we can go no further."

"I'll have a word with Colonel Zalik." Vesper turned on her heel and marched back into the headquarters.

"The *Lincilla* is bold, *effendi.*" Nilo gazed after her. "We have a proverb: Brave heart and fair face can walk through the bramblebush without a scratch."

Vesper soon rejoined us. From her expression, the bramblebush had not been cooperative.

"Zalik himself ordered our coach impounded. He must have done it while I was writing my letter. He claimed our papers only applied to us and didn't include a vehicle."

"Nothing more is possible, then." Nilo sighed ruefully. "We cannot go against a Zentan's command."

"I won't go against it," said Vesper. "I'll go around it."

She whistled through her teeth at the driver of a passing wagon and strode over to bargain with him about taking us the remaining miles to Alba-Collia. The man nodded and beckoned to us.

However, before Nilo could shoulder our baggage, two police officers hurried up. They had, apparently, been observing Vesper from across the street. They spoke briefly to the wagoner, who hastily slapped the reins and rattled away with all speed.

"They told the driver he'd be arrested if he carried us anywhere," said Vesper. "Also by order of Colonel Zalik. What's more, they said there's a law against loitering in the street."

The police officers had sauntered back to the corner, where they stood watching our every move.

"Pick up the baggage," said Vesper. "I don't think there's a law against using our legs."

We limped into Alba-Collia under a maliciously blazing sun. The place turned out to be little more than an up-country hamlet: an unpaved central square, clusters of timbered dwellings, a smithy, and the ever-present *kaffenion*, with chairs and tables set out in the middle of the walkway so passersby had to edge around or through them. A handful of oldsters sunned themselves, played chess or dominoes, which seemed the extent of local activity. Beyond, the Petrosias towered in great crags.

Nilo found rooms for us on the second floor of the *kaffenion*. That is, he found us something like broom closets. Except for the occasional horse trader or grain dealer, Alba-Collia was hardly a magnet for visitors and offered scant provision for them. I could not imagine why Holly had been interested in it. I said as much to Vesper.

"That's why we're here," she answered. "To find out."

I begged leave to rest. While Vesper and Nilo went off to look around the village, I cooled my feet in a bucket of water—the nearest approach to a bathtub the landlord had available. I napped until late afternoon on a mattress as craggy as the Petrosias.

Vesper had not yet returned, so I ventured downstairs for a cup of the hair-raising Illyrian coffee. My glance happened to fall on a group of young men playing cards at one of the tables.

It took a few moments for me to realize that, in fact, they were not playing cards, neither laying down nor picking up, but merely holding them. Their attention centered, rather, on a big, broad-shouldered fellow, leaning his face in his hand and talking intently to his tablemates.

Something about him struck me as familiar. I racked my memory without result. Finally, I decided I was mistaken. I went back to my coffee. A little later, glancing up again, I noticed the chairs were empty, the cards abandoned.

Vesper arrived just then, sighted me, and hurried to my table.

"Nilo's gone to see if he can get some equipment for us. There's no telling when ours will turn up. I won't hold my breath waiting for it."

I suddenly remembered. The man talking to the card players—I had seen him days before; he had been with a young woman. Did Vesper recall them?

"Milan and Silvia," said Vesper.

Exactly so. I told her that Milan had chosen to favor Alba-Collia with his presence.

"Are you sure?" Vesper raised an eyebrow. "He's a long way from that village where we met him. I expect Nilo will be glad to see him."

Master Nilo, I suggested, would do better to earn his keep than hang around with his cronies.

"Don't worry about that," said Vesper. "None of us will do much hanging around. As soon as Nilo finds some good horses, we'll ride upland. Nilo says the villagers believe the mountains are haunted by the ghosts of Vartan's fallen warriors.

"He tells me Vartan fought his last battle right here. Most everything in the countryside is named after him. The Silvana Forest is Vartan's Woods, Lake Lara is Vartan's Well."

Interesting, I agreed, but I pointed out that none of this gave us any clue to the magical army.

"Not yet," said Vesper, "but it's a place to start."

Nilo, meantime, had drifted into the *kaffenion* and slouched, uninvited, into a chair beside Vesper.

"I have spoken with Matrona Mira," he announced. "She will see you as soon as she is able."

"She's the village herb woman," explained Vesper. "The nearest thing to a doctor between here and Vitora."

Alarmed, I asked if Vesper was ailing.

"It's not for medicine. For stories. Matrona Mira's the village storyteller, too. I want to talk to her about the *Illyriad*. She must know those tales, and she might help us."

Vesper broke off then. A band of boys and girls had come into the square. Their arrival stirred great interest among the *kaffenion* patrons, who cheered and waved as the youngsters pranced by.

They were, indeed, kicking up their heels like colts, all very high-spirited. Prancing and curvetting along with them was a white horse.

Vesper, charmed by the sight, clapped her hands and showed as much enthusiasm as the villagers.

"Vartan's horse," Nilo explained. "It is an old custom.

A horse must be always ready and waiting for him when he returns. Each year, the finest animal is chosen. They will soon hold the festival."

"What festival?" Vesper asked.

"It is only a small village celebration, of no importance." Nilo shrugged. "A little bonfire, a little dancing."

"That must be it." Vesper's face lit up. "Brinnie, don't you remember? My father wrote about a horse festival. You thought it was a livestock fair." She turned to Nilo. "Lucky we got here in time. We'll have to see it."

"Ah, well, *Lincilla,* that is not possible." Nilo hemmed and hawed, uncomfortable and apologetic.

"Of course it is," Vesper said. "We're here, aren't we? And so's the festival."

"It is only for the villagers, *Lincilla,* not outsiders. *Farenkis*— no. They would be unwelcome. I am sorry. You must stay away from it."

"Nonsense," said Vesper. "We won't bother anyone."

"You must not go," Nilo said abruptly. "*Lincilla,* promise you will not."

"Don't worry." Vesper smiled. "I understand."

Nilo looked relieved. But I also understood. Vesper had not promised anything at all.

As was to be expected, Nilo had done absolutely nothing about finding new gear for us. I took that duty on myself and managed to lay hands on some ropes, candles, sheets of canvas, and other items I thought would be most useful. It was sundown by the time I finished shopping and returned to the *kaffenion.* The patrons had gone indoors. From halfway down the street, I could hear a strange commotion.

I hurried inside to see a good number of villagers crowded around a table. A chair had been set up on top of it. On the chair perched Vesper.

"Look what I found," she called, holding up a *dombra*. "An Illyrian banjo!"

At that, she started plunking happily away with the villagers' wholehearted encouragement. I would have preferred seeing Vesper behave with a little more decorum, but the dear girl was so thoroughly enjoying the occasion that I did not wish to interfere.

I squeezed onto a bench while Vesper favored the company with several American airs, which the Illyrians thought were marvelous, clapping and stamping after each one.

Then, to my astonishment, Nilo scrambled up and took her place. He gave voice to a few songs, mainly about turtledoves and fountains. He was surprisingly good. In addition to old Illyrian proverbs, playing the *dombra* counted among his only discernible talents. Then a villager replaced him, and it was turn and turn about, with good-natured boisterousness and, occasionally, broken crockery.

The songs were sometimes rousing and sometimes melancholy, and seemed to have fifty verses each. After a while, I began yawning and stole off to my broom closet.

The merrymakers finally tired. I dropped into a sound sleep—until a ferocious knocking jolted me out of my cot. Vesper was calling me. I heard the landlord add his urgent voice.

I flung open the door, to be faced with a pair of Zentan police officers.

"Zalik's orders again." Vesper elbowed past the officers. The landlord was making swimming motions of distress. "They'll shut down the *kaffenion* if we're allowed to stay."

The landlord stammered apologies. His livelihood was at stake, he begged us to leave immediately. Nilo, lurking in the background, edged forward.

"*Lincilla,* come with me," he whispered. "I shall see to everything."

The officers stood by as we packed and kept a hard eye on us until we were in the street, bag and baggage—by now a familiar condition. It was barely dawn. Colonel Zalik, I remarked, had a curious way of looking after us.

"That blubberous lump." Vesper snorted. "He's out to get us. So far, he's done pretty well."

I did not see why Colonel Zalik would have any personal interest in making our lives miserable.

"Neither do I," said Vesper. "That bothers me. What's he up to?"

We trudged along in the half-light, following Nilo. Vesper continued chewing over possible reasons for Zalik's determination to make nomads of us.

"Regulations, doing his duty, protecting us—that's hogwash," said Vesper. "We're in his backyard, and he wants us out."

It did seem to be the case. I was confident, however, that King Osman would soon set matters right. We had, by now, plodded our way to the village outskirts. Nilo halted at some ramshackle farm buildings. Whether he knew the owner or was simply making free with other people's property, I felt too sleepy to care. He conducted us to a barn and stables, and lodged us in vacant stalls.

"No one will trouble you here," he said. "When the wolf howls, the lambs hide."

Nilo went off then. I settled down as comfortably as I could. From the aroma, I suspected my quarters harbored goats, a suspicion confirmed when several of the creatures wandered in and made themselves at home.

Vesper soon came into my stall. Instead of catching up on her sleep, she had explored the barn. She carried a bundle of clothing.

"There's a lot of these hidden under the straw." She held up a garment.

It was a Zentan cavalry uniform.

"What do you make of it, Brinnie?"

I replied that I made it none of our business. I strongly suggested putting the thing immediately back where she found it.

Before she could do so, Nilo returned with a pile of blankets. Vesper showed him her discovery. Nilo examined it, frowning uneasily.

"*Lincilla,* I think you must forget you ever found this. Illyrians have their ways of dealing with Zentans. It will be wiser for all of us to ask no questions."

He threw aside the uniform as if it might attack him, and produced a flask of goat's milk and some chunks of black bread. Vesper, as usual, was ravenous. She munched away, then stopped suddenly between bites.

"Nilo—I meant to tell you. Brinnie saw Milan."

"Here? Milan is in Alba-Collia?"

The news seemed to impress him. He asked me for more details, but I could tell him nothing beyond my brief glimpse in the *kaffenion.*

"You didn't know he was coming here?" asked Vesper.

Nilo shook his head. "Milan—we do not ask where he goes or what he does."

He left us to ourselves then, after reminding Vesper to forget about the uniforms.

She chose to ignore his advice. "I remember Zalik said something about his men being attacked and having their uniforms taken. I'm trying to work out exactly when that happened."

I did not see what difference it made.

"It could make a very interesting difference," replied Vesper. "Those troopers who escorted us said they'd fought a band of rebels, didn't they?"

Yes, I said, we had seen them galloping through the town and had run into them soon after the battle. They had left us near Vitora to go after another rebel band. The

Illyrians must have turned the tables on them, taken their clothes, and tied them to trees.

"There's another way to look at it," said Vesper. "Suppose—just suppose the troopers had their uniforms taken *before* we met them. All we know is what they told us. They said they'd won. What if they'd lost?"

Had that been the case, I answered, they could not have been riding with us.

"True," said Vesper. "If they really were Zentans."

"Dear girl," I said, "they spoke Zentan, they frightened the wits out of Nilo— What else could they have been?"

"Illyrians. Rebels in disguise."

That, I said, was extremely unlikely. If they were Illyrian rebels, why would they have gone to the trouble of escorting us?

Vesper shrugged. "I don't know. I just wondered about it."

She said no more and went to put back the uniform. I pulled the blanket over my head and enjoyed a morning nap under the watchful eyes of the goats.

Nilo, for once, turned out to be right. Zalik's men did not trouble us. The *bimbashi* had either lost track of our whereabouts or had lost interest in harassing us. The next couple of days were quiet. The goats and I came to friendly terms, Vesper continued poking here and there around the village. I did not see Milan again. Nilo did not mention him, so I assumed that worthy had gone elsewhere.

We still had no word of our *firman* and equipment. Distasteful though the prospect was, I thought I should ride to Vitora and speak with Colonel Zalik.

"Let sleeping whales lie," said Vesper. "Stir him up and he'll start on us again. We have something better to do. Matrona Mira can see us tonight. It isn't far. Nilo's coming along to show us the way."

That evening, I was prepared to meet an old hag full of folkish superstitions and humbug, doddering in a hovel, mumbling incantations and old Illyrian proverbs.

Her dwelling was no hovel, nor was the *matrona* a hag. Though undoubtedly old, her face a spiderweb of wrinkles, she was a vigorous, bright-eyed little woman. She did not dodder, she bustled. After Nilo made all the properly ceremonious introductions, she popped in and out of one of the curtained alcoves off the main room to fetch cups of herb tea, then popped in and out of another little chamber, attending to some unfinished household task.

Vesper and Matrona Mira struck it off well from the first moment. Vesper sat beside her on a bench near the fireplace. The bunches of dried herbs hanging from the rafters gave the room a pleasant fragrance. The *matrona* listened closely while Vesper explained the purpose of our journey.

"That is Zentan lore, not Illyrian," the *matrona* said when Vesper asked for information about Ahmad's magical army. "We have many tales of Vartan, but few dealing with his enemies.

"There is one I remember, but I fear it has nothing to do with what you seek."

"Even so," said Vesper, "I'd like to hear it."

The *matrona* made a gesture with her hand—a graceful, sweeping movement, giving me the odd sensation that she was wiping away the present moment and reaching back into a distant past. She spoke in a low but clear voice, occasionally using antiquated words which Nilo translated.

"In Vartan's day, a day which will come again," the *matrona* began, "three Zentan princes sought to learn the secret of his strength.

"Bearing a chest of treasure, hoping that offering riches would sway him, they journeyed to Vartan's Castle.

"Before they reached it, wolves barred their way through Vartan's Woods. The first Zentan led the creatures astray so the others might go on.

"When those two halted to quench their thirst from Vartan's Well, the second remained there, enchanted by the songs of the water sprites. The third pressed on alone, bearing the treasure chest.

"At last, he reached the castle. King Vartan welcomed him, gave him food and drink, and treated him with every courtesy. But when Vartan heard what the Zentan sought, he laughed and scorned the treasure.

" 'The secret of my strength has already been revealed to you,' said Vartan. 'It lies in my wolves and in all other beasts and birds in my forest. It lies in my well, as it does in all other springs and rivers. It lies in the stones of my castle, as it does in all hills and mountains.'

"At this, the Zentan understood that Vartan's strength could never be taken from him by mortal being. Honoring Vartan as the greatest king, the Zentan remained there and never journeyed home again.

"This was in Vartan's day, a day which will come again."

The tale, I found, was not very exciting or interesting, and more inscrutable than some of Nilo's proverbs.

Vesper held the opposite opinion. She thought the tale was fascinating. What intrigued her, though, was not the business of wolves and water sprites.

"Part of it reminds me of the *Illyriad*," Vesper said.

"Ahmad wanted to give Vartan a treasure. And here's a story about a Zentan bringing Vartan a treasure chest. The tales are different, but they both start with the same idea. Are they both telling about something that really happened?

"What about Vartan's Castle?" Vesper went on. "Was there ever such a thing?"

"Yes," the *matrona* said. "By Vartan's Well—as we call Lake Lara. It stands no longer. The tale goes that Vartan stirred in his sleep, the earth rumbled, the stones split, and the castle toppled into ruins."

Vesper would gladly have listened to more tales, but the *matrona* indicated that our visit was over and invited us to return some other day.

Vesper tried to help the old woman carry the cups and kettle into the alcove. The *matrona*, quite abruptly and firmly, steered Vesper away, thanked her nonetheless, and wished us a hasty good-night.

"That Zentan treasure sticks in my mind," said Vesper, as we made our way to our goat-ridden lodgings. "Not much of a clue, but the only clue we have. Nilo can take us to Lake Lara. We'll have a look at the castle."

"*Lincilla,*" put in Nilo, "I can tell you what you will find. Nothing. It is a waste of your time. Besides, it is difficult country. No one goes there."

"So much the better," said Vesper. "We'll be the first."

The prospect of actually doing some work must have alarmed Nilo. Before Vesper extracted a promise from him, he mumbled something about an errand and hurried off, leaving us to ourselves and the goats.

"I like the *matrona,*" Vesper said. "We'll visit her again. But—it's puzzling."

I agreed. The *matrona*'s tale had likely been originally an old nature myth, but now so changed that it was incomprehensible.

"I don't mean the story was puzzling," Vesper said. "Something else was odd. When I started into that alcove, I caught a glimpse of somebody. I think it was Silvia."

"Silvia was friendly enough, the time we met," Vesper said. "Why would she hide from us? Why didn't the *matrona* want me to see her?"

For one thing, I replied, Vesper was not sure it had been Silvia. For another, Silvia had every right to be where she pleased. For still another, there were a dozen good reasons for her to be in the *matrona*'s cottage.

"Name one," said Vesper.

That, I said, was beside the point. The principle remained the same.

Vesper did not pursue the question. She turned her thoughts to Lake Lara. We would, she decided, go exploring as soon as Nilo could pack all we needed.

Nilo, however, did not return to the stable. Next morning, we went looking for him in the village, expecting to find him loafing around the *kaffenion*. He was not there.

The proprietor could tell us nothing. He had been busy

carrying chairs and tables indoors, clearing a space on the walkway. The festival would take place that evening.

The villagers had already begun hanging garlands and bunches of evergreens at the house fronts. A crew of men and women piled kindling in the middle of the square.

Vesper observed these activities with curiosity. "Nilo said it would only be a little bonfire."

Nilo's sense of dimension, I told her, matched his sense of direction. Large or small, the bonfire did not concern us. Not only were we uninvited, Nilo had made it plain that we were unwelcome.

"That was when we first got here," said Vesper. "The villagers didn't know us then. We're friends now. They'd want us to join in."

I advised against it. In the holy city of Mecca, when our presence was discovered, her father and I had to run for our lives. Locals can be touchy about their privacy.

"The festival could be important. It's something we have to see," replied Vesper. "I'll talk to Nilo."

The elusive Nilo was nowhere to be found, though Vesper spent much of the day looking for him. The dear girl appeared noticeably distressed, not a customary state for her. She began her search again, still to no avail.

The simple fact was Nilo had vanished.

I assured Vesper he would pop up again when we needed him least. Meantime, heeding his caution against intruding, I looked forward to a quiet evening with the goats. Vesper had no such intention.

"We're going," she declared. "This isn't Mecca, it's Alba-Collia. They won't run us out of town."

I could not convince her otherwise. However, I did

insist on keeping well in the background, calling no attention to ourselves, and staying only briefly.

We waited until after dark, when we heard a babble of voices and the twanging of *dombras*. The bonfire already blazed, flames rising nearly to the rooftops, turning the square bright as day.

As for keeping in the background, Vesper decided we should be in the front rank.

"If we can't see anything, Brinnie, what's the use?"

Accordingly, Vesper led me sidling and squeezing through the crowd. The spectators laughed and called out to her, and in no way objected. The audience was large, including not only Alba-Collians but also throngs from the nearby hamlets.

"Zalik wasn't invited, I'm sure," said Vesper, "but he's sent a lot of his tin soldiers." She called my attention to the troops posted along the fringes of the crowd. "Most all of his constables, too."

The presence of the officers did not dampen the Illyrians' spirit. If anything, it produced the opposite effect. The locals joked among themselves, passing around leather flasks and taking hearty swigs of the contents, whistling, stamping their feet. But then, a few moments later, they fell absolutely silent.

A curious procession entered the square. In a way, it looked much like a school pageant, with some dozen villagers decked out in colorful but obviously homemade costumes. Masks painted with strange symbols covered their faces. They carried farm tools, sheaves of grain, pine boughs, or bunches of flowers. Some wore fur capes; others were only lightly clad.

Beyond an impression of something quite ancient, the significance of the procession escaped me.

Vesper carefully studied the participants. "Twelve people, twelve different emblems. The twelve months of the year."

"Dear girl, that's wonderful! Of course they are." It had never occurred to me, but Vesper's admirable intelligence had grasped the meaning immediately. I beamed at her.

Now, three women wearing flowing robes were borne in on something like a carnival float, which also served as a platform from which they observed the doings in the square.

"There's Matrona Mira." Vesper pointed to the eldest of the three. "Isn't she splendid? And that's the baker's daughter and the landlord's little girl."

The dozen villagers, meantime, had formed a circle around the fire. While the *dombras* twanged louder, with the added rattle and jingle of tambourines, the twelve began a graceful, intertwining dance. The steps were complex but, all in all, nicely executed.

The dancers withdrew after a while. The music grew wilder, and some of the bolder men and women broke from the crowd and raced back and forth through the flames of the bonfire. This I had no difficulty recognizing as a custom older than the Illyrians probably realized. From what I knew of similar pagan rites, I wondered if it were proper for Vesper to stay and watch them. Perhaps that was what Nilo had meant.

Cheers burst from the crowd. Vesper pointed to the far side of the square.

"Brinnie—there! Vartan's horse!"

A young girl, crowned with flowers, led in the spirited animal, unsaddled, with garlands around the neck and blossoms woven into mane and tail. Vesper clapped her hands, delighted. Girl and horse made a circuit, while the onlookers eagerly reached out, trying to touch the prancing steed.

Those moments were strangely and quite deeply moving. Otherwise, the festival was generally similar to many that Holly and I had witnessed, a harmless rustic celebration.

"It's charming," said Vesper. "I don't see why Zalik sent so many troops. What's he worried about?"

We understood all too soon.

From the crowd rose shouts of "Vartan! Vartan!" Voice after voice took up the cry.

"Vartan! Freedom! Vartan has come back!"

The shouts swelled to a furious tide. The charming rustic ritual was turning into open defiance, if not insurrection. Had the villagers gone mad? Did they expect the Zentan authorities to wink at such rebelliousness?

The police, indeed, did not intend to wink. Colonel Zalik must have foreseen the happening. In addition to the constables and soldiers, a large cavalry detachment had been stationed at the edge of the village. These reinforcements now came galloping toward the crowd.

The constables, at the same time, drove like a wedge through the mass of onlookers. The villagers, surely, would break and fall back. Instead, they rashly chose to make a fight of it. The dancers banded together, fending off the onslaught with their pageant implements. Elsewhere, knots of Illyrians engaged the Zentans with makeshift weapons— chairs and tables from the *kaffenion* and even a few *dombras*.

Vesper and I, by weight of numbers, had been flung

close to the bonfire. Contemplating the possibility of our ending up amid the flames, I cast around for an escape. But a number of officers had begun seizing whatever Illyrians they could lay hands on. We were not exempt.

As the officers set upon us, I politely explained that we were innocent bystanders, *farenkis* on a scholarly expedition. I emphasized our friendship with King Osman and assured the constables we had no part in the disturbance.

If my words were unconvincing, no doubt it was because Vesper, at that very moment, snatched a burning brand from the fire and began swinging away at any approaching Zentan, stoutly defending Matrona Mira beside her.

The officers swarmed over us, seizing Vesper and the *matrona*, collaring me as well. Along with a number of Illyrians, we were half dragged, half carried from the square, Vesper struggling all the while.

As the fighting behind us sharpened, we were manhandled into a wagon and borne off under guard in the direction of Vitora.

"Dear girl," I cried, "what's happening to us?"

"If I had to guess," replied Vesper, "I'd say we've been arrested."

# CHAPTER

## ❧ 10 ❧

"I hope Nilo's all right," Vesper said. "Lucky thing he wasn't in the village."

Master Nilo, I replied, was undoubtedly loafing in some quiet corner. Wherever he was, he was better off than we were. Our feckless *dragoman* must have sniffed trouble in the wind and made himself scarce.

"He told us not to go," Vesper reminded me.

For that, I had no answer. My immediate concern, in any case, was for Vesper and how to deal with the regrettable fix we had fallen into so unwittingly. I tried to look on the brighter side. As I told Vesper, considering the turmoil in Alba-Collia, we were safer out of there.

"And into Zalik's lockup?" returned Vesper. "Don't count on a gracious welcome."

I disagreed. Whatever my personal opinion of him, Colonel Zalik was a military officer of high rank, with a strong sense of duty. I was confident he would do everything he could.

"I'm sure he will," said Vesper.

She turned her attention to the *matrona*. Squeezed though we were in this jolting Zentan equivalent of a police van, and possibly facing criminal charges, Vesper took the occasion to inquire about Silvia.

"Didn't I see her that night in your cottage?"

The *matrona* nodded. "Yes. She had suffered an injury. I treated her and gave her a place to rest."

"Silvia had an accident? Was she badly hurt?"

"She is well recovered," said the *matrona*. "She left soon after you."

"What happened?" Vesper pressed on. "What kind of accident? Did she come to Alba-Collia with Milan?"

The *matrona* gave only the vaguest answers. Vesper would have kept on nosing into an obviously private matter, but by then, we had reached Vitora and were heading toward the center of town, and the conversation was interrupted by a sudden commotion.

The driver halted instantly. There were sharp volleys of rifle fire. The cavalry escort galloped for Colonel Zalik's headquarters, which seemed to be the source of the shooting. The driver and the guards seized their weapons, leaped from the wagon, and raced after the horsemen.

The Illyrian prisoners snatched the opportunity to scramble down and scatter in all directions. Two of them had picked up the *matrona* and, between them, were practically carrying her bodily away.

Vesper, too, had jumped out. I clambered after her. She

began pulling my arm, urging me to follow the escaping Illyrians.

That, I tried to explain, was the last thing in the world we should do. We were in trouble enough without becoming fugitives from justice, declared criminals, hunted by Zalik's police.

"I'd rather be hunted than caught." Vesper tugged all the harder.

We had no time to continue our discussion. A band of horsemen came dashing straight at us. Some brandished rifles, others led pack animals loaded with boxes and sacks, and all of them whooped and hallooed like madmen, yelling ferociously in Illyrian, which made their war cries all the more bloodcurdling.

On their heels galloped a detachment of Zalik's cavalry —not a great number, since most had been dispatched to Alba-Collia. Nevertheless, they sharply engaged the Illyrians, who wheeled their mounts to confront them.

These Illyrians must be the rebels whom Zalik had warned against.

Shouts of "Vartan! Vartan!" rose around us. Despite Vesper's reluctance, I tried to remove her from the fray. By now, unfortunately, we were caught in the midst of plunging hooves and of Illyrians and Zentans grappling each other, firing in complete disregard for innocent bystanders —namely, Vesper and me—or slashing furiously with sabers or wicked-looking Illyrian blades.

I tried to gain the attention of a Zentan rider, hoping he might get us clear of our predicament. Without so much as pausing to ask who I was, he brought up a long-barreled pistol and aimed straight at me.

Vesper sprang forward in a flash. She seized the fellow

by one leg, heaved with all her might, and toppled him out of the saddle. His shot went astray while he himself pitched headlong to the ground, a foot entangled in the stirrup. His mount bolted away, dragging him cursing and struggling down the street.

This happened so quickly it took me a few moments to realize the dear girl had saved my life, or kept me from serious injury. I had no time to express gratitude.

In that fraction of a second, as I turned a Zentan brought a rifle butt down on my head, after which, I was aware of nothing else.

When I opened my eyes again, I thought my vision was blurred. I realized it was dawn mist. The air was sharp and chilly, the fragrance of pine almost overpowering. As best I could tell, I lay in a grassy clearing. Tethered nearby, horses cropped the turf. A handful of Illyrians loitered about in the bluish haze.

Vesper sat cross-legged on the ground beside me. She smiled fondly. "Don't worry, Brinnie. You're definitely alive. You had a hard knock, but nothing's broken. You'll be fine."

Vesper had been munching on a slab of black bread, which she offered me. I did not feel up to breakfast. The full truth of our situation struck me with alarm.

"How did we come here?" I tried to climb to my feet. "These people are dangerous rebels, those maniacs fighting in Vitora—"

"They took us with them," said Vesper. "I asked them to."

"You did what?" My head started pounding worse than ever.

"It was either that or jail. They unloaded a packhorse so they could tie you to its back."

That, I said, was very thoughtful of them. I trusted they would now be kind enough to return us to civilization.

"That hasn't been decided yet," said Vesper. "I don't think they mean us any harm. But what they do with us is up to Vartan."

"He's here?" I cried. "Vartan himself?"

"He planned the whole thing. He counted on Zalik sending most of his men into the village. Then Vartan and his people swooped down on Vitora, broke into the armory and storehouses, and made off with all they could carry. It worked perfectly. It was one of his best raids. That's what Silvia tells me. She was in Vitora."

Silvia a rebel? I thought of Milan. Surely he was one. Now I understood why he and his cronies had been loitering around the village.

"Silvia told me about the Zentan uniforms, too," added Vesper. "I was right. The Illyrians ambushed those cavalrymen just outside of town and took their clothes and horses.

"That was another of Vartan's plans. Very clever, I'd say. What safer way to travel? The Zentan patrols never gave them a second look. But Silvia was wounded during the ambush, and they took her to Alba-Collia. Matrona Mira patched her up. The *matrona* keeps a sort of hospital and hiding place for Vartan's people."

The old *matrona*? Illyrian rebels were popping up everywhere. I explained to Vesper that we did not dare be further mixed up with them. If King Osman found out, we could hardly convince him we had not been deliberately consorting with his enemies. We must escape as soon as possible.

"I wouldn't try it," said Vesper.

Silvia strode up then, ordering us to make ready. I pleaded that I was in no condition to travel. She and her friends would not take it amiss if we stayed behind and looked after ourselves? Silvia gave me a hard glance. I did not press the subject.

Vesper, in any case, was in excellent spirits as we mounted and set off again. The sun was up, it turned her hair bright orange; in her Illyrian garb, she appeared altogether at home amid the steepening hills. She jogged along, sniffing the spicy air, admiring the peaks rising ahead, chatting with Silvia beside her.

The Illyrians, however, allowed little opportunity to appreciate the scenery. They kept pushing the pace, eager to join their comrades. The rebels, I gathered, had separated into smaller bands. Some had gone ahead, some followed. All were to meet higher up in the Petrosias.

When the ground became too broken, we had to dismount and pick our way up rocky inclines. We skirted Vartan's Steps—huge slabs of granite stripped bare by wind and weather—and continued climbing. I asked Vesper if she thought they were taking us all the way to Mount Albor.

"I hope so," she cheerfully replied. "We might do some exploring."

The Illyrians, however, halted on a wide and level shelf jutting from the mountainside.

"Brinnie, it's practically a village," Vesper exclaimed. As she pointed out, the area indeed swarmed with people. Men and women trundled kegs and crates, or sorted stacks of weapons. Cook fires burned here and there. At the horse lines, some rough-looking fellows tended the animals. It was a beehive of activity, almost literally, for the slopes were honeycombed with caves and recesses of varying size. In front of one, somebody had even hung out laundry.

"This must be Vartan's stronghold," said Vesper. "Amazing! I mean, it's amazing they'd let us see the place. That's a secret they wouldn't want let out. I suppose they trust us to keep our mouths shut. Or they don't expect we'll be leaving."

I did not care to reflect on that possibility. Vesper dismissed it. "We needn't worry. I'm sure Vartan will be reasonable. I'll explain it all to him."

Silvia conducted us into one of the larger caverns. It was full of Illyrians, squatting on the ground or stretched out sleeping. There were ammunition chests and stacks of rifles and sabers, the gains of the previous night.

In the midst of it all, glowering and scowling, sat Milan.

Vesper tried to pull me back, but I stepped up to him immediately.

"My dear Milan—Vartan, if you prefer," I began, "we are unfortunate victims of circumstance. We ask only to return quietly to Alba-Collia."

To my dismay, Milan paid no attention whatever. His eyes were elsewhere. At the same time, a cry from Vesper interrupted my plea. I turned. A new arrival had entered the cave.

"Nilo!" Vesper ran and embraced the wretch.

I was not as happy to see him. Forgetting our present danger, I had a few bones to pick.

"Scoundrel!" I flung at him. "We have been arrested, clubbed, kidnapped, our lives at risk—all thanks to you."

"*Effendi,* this is not my fault. If you and the *Lincilla* had only listened to me, if you had kept away from the festival, you would have been safe."

I wanted to hear none of that. He had saved his own skin, the least he could do was make an effort to save ours. He could vouch for us, assure our captors we would reveal nothing of their camp, convince Milan that we would go about our business, that he should release us here and now.

Nilo spread his hands. "Milan cannot decide that."

"That's true," put in Vesper.

Vartan, I replied, was leader of the rebels and his orders would certainly be obeyed.

"But Milan isn't the one," said Vesper. "Brinnie, you've got it mixed up. Am I right?" she added, turning to look squarely at Nilo.

The lout gave an exasperating grin and shrugged his shoulders. "Yes, *Lincilla.* I am Vartan."

"I thought so," Vesper said. "I just wanted to make sure."

"*Lincilla,* how could you have known?" Nilo looked at her with a mixture of astonishment and admiration.

"I had to guess a lot, and the guesses turned out to be right," said Vesper. "Little things here and there. For one, you showed up at the hotel just when we needed a *drago-man.* A neat coincidence? It might have been. Or might not."

"It was not," admitted Nilo. "We knew of your arrival in Zenta. Two *farenkis* are not easily overlooked, especially when one of them is so charming. We soon learned your destination."

"At first, I wondered if you were the one who tried to kill me in the Old Town, coming back to finish the job. That didn't fit very well. You wouldn't have waited, you'd have done it right away. So, you weren't an assassin. And you certainly weren't a *dragoman.*"

"I was not a good one?"

Vesper smiled at him. "You were—well, you were very likeable. Otherwise, you were a disaster. You couldn't have been a real *dragoman*.

"A spy for the Zentans?" Vesper went on. "I doubted that. You were truly anxious to get out of town. For some important reason. Why didn't you just pick up and go? Then, just to see how it worked, I imagined what someone would do if he had to travel safely for a long distance. There were a lot of possibilities. Including being a *dragoman* for two *farenkis* who were under royal protection. That fit nicely, with Milan, Silvia, maybe some others, keeping an eye on things along the way. A cavalry escort that turned out to be Illyrian rebels. You had to be one of Vartan's people. So important? So valuable? Vartan himself.

"It was a good guess," Vesper added. "Then, just now, as soon as you came in, everybody stopped talking and eating, and they all turned to look at you as if nothing would happen until you got here.

"Don't worry, Nilo. I won't tell anyone. Neither will Brinnie."

I stood there too bewildered to speak, let alone tell Nilo's secret. Or Vartan's secret. He had changed so suddenly and completely. His whole bearing was different. He had an air of easy authority, as if long accustomed to being obeyed. His eyes were sharper and harder now that he had thrown off the guise of a feckless layabout. He looked a little dangerous. I preferred him when he was feckless.

"One thing I still haven't figured out," said Vesper. "Who stabbed me?"

"I do not know," said Nilo, "and that, *Lincilla,* troubles me greatly."

Here, I broke in to say that a more immediate question was our getting back to Alba-Collia.

"And to Colonel Zalik?" said Nilo. "That would be unwise."

He drew a sheaf of papers from his jacket. "In Vitora, we took the opportunity to investigate the *bimbashi*'s office. We hoped to find information useful to us. We did. We also found these."

Vesper leafed through the papers which Nilo handed to her. "A receipt for our equipment—it got there the day before we did. My letter—never sent. A message from Osman, ordering Zalik to give us every assistance. And this."

She held up a document bearing the royal seal. "Our *firman*. He had it all the time."

"Zalik is your enemy, *Lincilla*. You must avoid him at all cost. The real question is, What shall you do now?"

I suggested handshakes all round, wishes of Godspeed and good luck, and we would make our way back to Zenta.

At this, Nilo hesitated. He frowned and bit his lips. "My people have put all their hope in Vartan. They will not betray me. I trust their silence. Can I trust yours?"

"You can," said Vesper. "You know that."

Nilo gave her a long glance. "Yes. I do know."

But there is always one in every group, whether the Ladies' Garden Committee or a meeting of cabinet ministers; once all is happily settled, some wretch has to point out what has been overlooked, raise questions, pick nits, and start the whole business up again. In this case, it was Milan.

"Remember this, Vartan," he said. "They are under the protection of the Zentan king. Are their loyalties with him?

He gave them a *firman*. Did they promise anything in exchange? What keeps them from telling Osman all they know of us? The word of a *farenki*—"

"The *Lincilla*'s word is enough," declared Nilo.

"You have it," Vesper said. "I'll do better than that. I think I can help you. Osman doesn't want Illyrians and Zentans at each other's throats. He told me that. I'm sure he meant it. His vizier's the one who's dead set against dealing with the Illyrians."

"It comes to the same. The Zentans wish to destroy us. But every Illyrian will fight against them."

"And get killed?" returned Vesper. "It doesn't have to be that way."

"How else, *Lincilla*?"

"Work out some agreement that suits both of you. I'll talk with Osman. Not his vizier. Osman himself. I know he'd be willing to grant—"

"Grant?" broke in Nilo. "Osman willing to grant?"

Vesper had touched a sore spot. Until now, Nilo had seemed interested. Vesper had not reckoned on the Illyrian temperament.

"Shall we beg a Zentan king to do us a favor?" Nilo angrily went on. "Graciously deign to grant what is already ours by right? We do not plead, *Lincilla*. We do not entreat. Our honor is worth more to us than a tyrant's charity. We beg for nothing. We take what is ours."

Nilo's eyes blazed as he held forth about honor, justice, freedom, and shedding blood in a noble cause. The fellow did have a way about him. He impressed me—as long as I did not think about what he was actually saying. He would have been magnificent had he been living in the twelfth century, a paladin out of the *Illyriad*, worthy to be Vartan himself. Given the ways of modern diplomacy, I calculated he was about seven hundred years too late.

He cooled down a bit after that. As for us, nothing could be decided at the moment. It was, Nilo explained, unlikely that Zalik would risk sending troops into the Petrosias, where he would be at a serious disadvantage, but he would harass the villagers for a while. Whatever we did, we must wait until things grew calmer.

Nilo and Milan stalked out of the cave then, talking intently between themselves.

"We'll have to stay here, Brinnie," said Vesper, undismayed at the prospect. "They're stuck with us."

No, I corrected, we were stuck with them, on the wrong side of the law.

"That depends on which side you think is right," Vesper said. "Isn't it odd— Osman says he'll bestow justice but won't let it be forced from him. Nilo's just the same. He won't accept anything that seems like a gift; he'd rather take it by force, for the sake of his honor. The more Nilo pushes, the more Osman will dig in his heels; and the more Nilo digs in his heels, the harder Osman will fight him. They're pulling at opposite ends of the same rope. What they'll end up with is a knot."

We settled down as best we could. Over the next few days, Nilo was often absent, but his followers kept arriving at the cave, staying briefly, disappearing again. They were, in all honesty, not a bad sort. They good-naturedly shared everything with us and made sure we were comfortable— that is, no more uncomfortable than they were.

Vesper enchanted them. She learned their names,

laughed and joked with them, and plunked a *dombra* one of them had brought. To pass idle moments, she played dominoes or the Illyrian version of mumblety-peg, borrowing a nasty-looking blade from one of the rebels. Somebody produced a chess set, which delighted her. She took on Nilo, when he happened to be in residence, and trounced him at every match.

"I wonder why they never let us out of the cave together?" she said to me.

I, too, had observed that Vesper was obliged to stay behind when I strolled for air and exercise, Milan keeping a hard eye on me from the shrubbery. Silvia always accompanied Vesper.

"Are they being careful of us?" Vesper added. "Or don't they really trust us?"

For all that, she was not impatient to leave. One day, however, coming back from a walk, I found her sitting with the chessboard on her lap, turning the pieces around and around in her fingers.

"It's interesting," she said. "Illyrian sets are all carved alike. It's traditional. The pawns are Zentan and Illyrian archers. The bishops, viziers. The kings are supposed to be Vartan and Ahmad. . . ."

She put the two pieces facing each other on the board and studied them intently. "They fought each other centuries ago, and they're still at it. Osman's going to send an army against Nilo. . . ."

She stopped and looked at me most forlornly. "It isn't a game, though. Nilo could be— They could all be killed."

I did not wish to answer. I had seen bands like Nilo's in Greece, in Crete, in Sicily. They all had the same look, all desperately brave and devoted. Sometimes, like Garibaldi's people, they won a little. Usually, they ended up nobly dead or drifted into banditry, having fought so long they forgot why they had started in the first place. Naturally, they were very young, but that was no fault of theirs.

"I never thought of people really getting killed before. Someone you know, someone—" Vesper suddenly put her head against my shoulder. She did not cry, but the dear girl was certainly at the edge. "Brinnie—I want to be home."

I patted her arm without, I fear, providing much comfort. Mary would have done better. Vesper straightened up.

"No. I don't want to go home. Not until it's settled. I won't have Nilo getting himself killed. And we'll find what we came to find."

I had my own opinion about those two subjects, but I kept it to myself. The poor child was suffering a touch of nerves—the result, naturally, of being more or less confined to a cave, subsisting on cheese and fiery hot sausages, being surrounded by desperate characters, including the most dangerous man in Illyria. It was no kind of life for a Philadelphian.

# ❧ 12 ❧

"I don't care what Nilo says about not accepting favors," Vesper told me later. "As soon as we're back in Zenta, I'll have a long talk with Osman. Somebody has to start listening to reason."

The possibility of reaching Zenta before the fighting broke out struck me as dim. More likely, we would become permanent residents of the cave and eat sausages the rest of our lives. Nilo did not intend to release us.

"This is the safest place, *Lincilla*," he said when he returned after nearly a week's absence. "Zalik has been looking for you even harder than he is looking for Vartan.

"I can stay no longer," he continued. "I have work to do in other villages. Milan and Silvia will come with me. You must wait here, *Lincilla*. You will be well cared for."

"No," said Vesper. "We're going with you. We can

help each other. I want to go to Zenta. You want to go—wherever you have to. There's a way to do both.

"Can you get hold of horses and a carriage? A wagon? Then do what you did before. Be our *dragoman*. Milan and Silvia can wear Zentan uniforms and ride along as our escort. We have our *firman*, we have a letter from Osman. They're very impressive documents; no one will question them. Once you're where you want to be, we'll separate and go our own ways."

"We have no uniforms," Nilo said. "The *bimbashi*'s men found them. They confiscated your baggage, too. As for the rest of your plan—" He rubbed his chin and thought for several moments. "Yes. It is a good one. It will serve your purpose and ours. Milan will see to everything we need."

"One more thing," said Vesper. "I'm not going to Zenta without a look at Vartan's Castle. It's important and I may not have another chance. The *matrona* said it was by Lake Lara. That's not far from here."

"You will find nothing of interest," said Nilo. "Only ruins."

"Then it won't take long to see them. We have to go in that direction anyway. We'll need to stop for a rest. We might as well do it there."

Milan looked doubtful. I felt the same. Our situation was touchy enough without adding a side trip. Nilo and Milan spoke apart for a while.

"*Lincilla*," said Nilo, after they finished, "we have an old proverb. The bear gladly trades a few grapes for the fox's pomegranates. When you offer me a service in Vartan's cause, I cannot refuse a small favor in your own."

"I hoped you'd see it that way," said Vesper.

We started next day at first light, leading our horses down the rocky slopes. Milan, Silvia, and a few others had already gone. They would meet us a safe distance from Alba-Collia with whatever vehicle they could obtain.

Now that he had stopped playing incompetent *dragoman*, Nilo proved an excellent guide. He knew the area, his shortcuts were as short as he claimed. By midday, we had our first view of Lake Lara shining silver blue in a little valley.

"I can imagine water sprites living here. A perfect setting for them," said Vesper. "No wonder that Zentan prince in Matrona Mira's story was spellbound. But we'd better not let it happen to us."

She pressed eagerly on, Nilo matching her pace. I caught up with them at the summit of a high, grassy mound. There, overlooking the lake, stood Vartan's Castle.

"It's magnificent," Vesper said in a hushed voice.

What I saw was a large heap of rubble.

"Magnificent—if you look at it the way it must have been." Vesper began striding toward the ruins. "You have to rebuild it in your mind, Brinnie."

Nilo and I followed as she scrambled over broken pillars that lay like stumps or fallen tree trunks. Vesper examined a fragment.

"Marble? That's not local stone, is it? It must have been hauled—who knows how far?"

Vesper went on enthusiastically, estimating the height of the pillars, where they had stood, and in effect, restoring the building in her imagination and making it take shape there before us.

"But—it's not a castle. The pillars must have stood—there, to make a portico. These broken slabs were steps

83

leading up to it. A fortress wouldn't have that kind of architecture. I think it must have been a temple."

Vesper was correct. What had been the central portion was overgrown with myrtle and laurel; it seemed to have caved in on itself. But, as Vesper pointed out, it was a temple, far too elaborate to be a simple rustic shrine. The structure would have been rectangular, with pillars on all sides to form graceful arcades.

"What could have destroyed it?" said Vesper. "Damage like that—I'd say, an earthquake."

Probably so. As I recalled my history, the region had suffered tremors at the same time as the catastrophic Lisbon earthquake of more than a hundred years ago. Illyrian folk-lore gave credit to Vartan stirring in his sleep.

"This is older than the *Illyriad*," Vesper went on. "From what I've studied about architecture, people didn't build like this in the twelfth century. It goes a lot farther back. Do you realize what that means? There was a civilization here long before Vartan. That's an important discovery in itself."

It was regrettable, I said, that we had no time to investigate thoroughly. There might well be a substructure: the private quarters of the priesthood, storage chambers, perhaps a special sanctum forbidden to all but those initiated in the secret ritual. I should have bitten my tongue.

"There's more belowground?" exclaimed Vesper. "How can we get in?"

We could not. The temple was in a state of collapse. Even if we found an entry, the structure had been weakened and might fall about our ears. For a safe and proper exploration, we required timbers, a framework, posts to shore up the excavation.

"Still," said Vesper, "it can't hurt to look around."

Disregarding my advice, she clambered over the ruins, poking here and there, scrabbling at loose rocks. Nilo caught her enthusiasm, and the pair set about probing every nook and cranny.

Vesper finally sang out that she had found something.

At the end of what had been the portico, a broken pillar lay across a gap in the flooring. She ran to the fringe of trees and soon came back, dragging a couple of long branches.

"Come lend a hand, Brinnie."

With Nilo's help, she began levering one end of the pillar while I prized up the other. The work put us all in a fine sweat, but we did at last roll aside the marble blockade. Vesper dropped to her knees and peered into a jagged opening a couple of feet across. She tossed a handful of rubble into the shaft.

"I can't tell how far it goes, but it seems clear. Let's take a look."

Nilo fetched a coil of rope and a lantern from his pack. I kept pointing out that we all had urgent business elsewhere, but Vesper's curiosity was aroused, and I finally gave in. The sooner she was satisfied, the sooner we would be on our way. Having had some experience with Holly in this kind of work, I thought it wiser for me to go first. Vesper refused to hear of it. While Nilo secured one end of his line around the pillar, Vesper lashed the other into a harness. She hooked the lantern to her belt and disappeared into the shaft.

Nilo and I waited anxiously. After a few minutes, I heard Vesper's muffled voice calling excitedly. Insisting it was my duty to be with her, I left Nilo stationed at the rim of the opening while I inched my way down.

The shaft was more or less free of debris, and widened

as I descended. Vesper was waiting, lantern in hand. She hurried me along a low-ceilinged passage of stone and timber construction—in reasonably good condition, considering the damage at ground level. Several chambers opened into this little corridor, but they had been mostly blocked by rubble.

"I didn't take time to look around much," Vesper said, leading me into a fairly large and unobstructed room. She strode to a ledge at the farther wall and raised the lantern. "But—Brinnie, you have to see this."

To my astonishment, I glimpsed a row of wooden figures, superbly carved, ornamented with gold and silver, studded with gems. These statuettes stood nearly a foot tall. Each bore some tool or implement. Their masklike faces held an expression of supernatural calm.

"Do you recognize them, Brinnie? They're like those dancers in the village. There—up above—three women, just as at the festival. How old would you say?"

I could only guess: well over a thousand years. They were unquestionably ancient.

"The folk in Alba-Collia must have been going through that ceremony for so long they've forgotten how or where it began."

Vesper's face shone with excitement. Justifiably. We had —that is, she had—stumbled on an example of a long-vanished, unsuspected Illyrian culture. The temple and its mysterious figures were enough to keep scholars busy for years. The whole area might yield all manner of treasures.

But Vesper had not finished. She drew me into what appeared to be an anteroom. Here, my foot struck something, and I cried out.

The sight of a skeleton, no matter how ancient, has always been unsettling to me. This one on the ground was not quite a skeleton; the dry air had preserved it and its garments quite well. Still, the fellow was not in good condition. I would gladly have parted company with him.

Vesper had no such queasiness. She drew my attention to what remained of richly embroidered robes and turban-like headgear.

"He's not Illyrian. He's Zentan. He's dressed like the pictures in my old *Illyriad*. But what was a Zentan doing in an Illyrian temple?"

She pointed to a sword nearby—the typical slender, curved Zentan blade. Another figure sprawled on the ground. A third, still clutching his weapon, had fallen next to it.

"What happened here? There must have been an awful fight." Vesper glimpsed an object on the stone floor. She picked it up. "An Illyrian archer!"

She scrambled over the ground. "Here's another. A Zentan, this time. And more of them, scattered every-where. Brinnie, they're chess pieces—but look at the size of them!"

She held up a handsomely wrought piece in the form of a grand vizier, easily a foot high, an impressive work of craftsmanship, then resumed her search.

"Most of the set's here," she said after a short while. "No—the Zentan king's missing. I found Vartan, but not Ahmad. That's odd."

She broke off suddenly and thought for some moments. "Brinnie, let's say the magical army is folklore. But what if something real got changed into a legend? Wouldn't you call chessmen a kind of army? Could Ahmad's gift have been a chess set? A royal game, a royal present from one king to another?"

Nilo was calling urgently. Reluctant to leave her discoveries and vowing to come back for a longer look, Vesper hurried down the passage and shinnied up the rope. Less nimble, I waited until she and Nilo hauled me to the surface.

Nilo, in some agitation, was pointing down the slope. Some pack mules had come into sight, along with a number of men bearing hand tools. Our horses had been tethered on the far side of the mound and thus went unobserved by what appeared to be a Zentan work party.

Nilo motioned us to crouch behind the bushes. A couple of the Zentans began spreading out sheets of canvas for a tent, while another set up a camp chair and folding table. Moments later, a horseman joined them, dismounted and glanced around, issuing instructions.

I jumped to my feet, surprised and delighted. Vesper was shouting something after me, but by then I was halfway down the slope, eager to greet this unexpected, though welcome, arrival.

# CHAPTER

## ❧ 13 ❧

"My dear Professor Garrett—really, this is quite extraordinary."

Dr. Helvitius shook my hand with intense cordiality. The scholar was dressed in very durable travel garments, a cloth cap covering much of his great shock of white hair, his feet encased in stout, knee-high boots. He appeared in the best of trim, hearty and vigorous. Clearly, he had not been sleeping in caves and living on overspiced sausages.

"But, good heavens, sir, what has happened to you?"

I could not, I told him, begin to describe our tribulations, nor could I adequately express my pleasure at finding a civilized individual.

"My unfortunate colleague, I must hear all the details of your harrowing journey. Will you take luncheon?" He gestured toward the table where one of his Zentan crew set out an array of victuals.

Vesper and Nilo had, by now, joined us. Nilo had

resumed his pose as humble *dragoman*. Except for a few scornful glances, the Zentans paid him no attention.

Vesper, surprisingly, behaved with almost impolite abruptness. Offering only minimal greetings, she demanded to know why he was here.

"For your own welfare, dear Miss Holly, and your guardian's." Helvitius was a little wounded by Vesper's attitude. "Our encounter is not accidental. I have spared no effort to find you. I only regret that I did not succeed before now."

"You've found us," said Vesper. "Why were you looking for us?"

"King Osman has been troubled, without word from you. His vizier is equally distressed. He has received news from Colonel Zalik of civil unrest, local disturbances, that you had vanished into thin air—perhaps met with misadventure. I took it on myself to learn what had befallen you."

"A lot has befallen us," replied Vesper. "Most of it thanks to Zalik."

Dr. Helvitius raised his eyebrows. "I am astonished to hear that. I met recently with the *bimbashi*. He impressed me as an excellent and diligent officer."

"That bald-headed crocodile," said Vesper, "has lied to us, robbed us, hounded us, tried to throw us in jail. Yes, I'd call that diligent."

"What alarming accusations," said Helvitius. "I do not understand."

"Neither do I." Vesper turned her glance on the camp furniture and the tent. "And I don't understand why you brought all this. Searching for us? You're setting up housekeeping."

"In addition to my concern for your well-being," said

Helvitius, "I hoped to join you in your field research. I found your enthusiasm and determination both admirable and intriguing. Your insistence on the reality of an impossible aspect of the *Illyriad*, I confess, aroused my curiosity. Like you, I wished to discover the facts."

"We've already done that."

Helvitius blinked. "Have you, indeed?"

I interrupted to explain that such was far from the case. Briefly, I told him of Vesper's notion. It was, of course, pure speculation. We had nothing to support it.

"Then let me share my own information with you." Dr. Helvitius invited us to seat ourselves, offered refreshments, and leaned back in his canvas chair. "As you know, it was my firm opinion that this so-called magical army was mere folkish fantasy. Yet, even the most learned may fall into error. As an honest researcher, I am duty bound to admit my mistake and correct it.

"Since our last meeting, I have examined evidence convincing me that this magical army has a basis in reality. Ahmad's promised gift to Vartan was, in fact, a set of chessmen."

"What made you change your mind so fast?" put in Vesper.

"I have been able to piece together certain details," Helvitius replied, "and form, to my complete satisfaction, a fairly clear picture of the historical events surrounding that episode. Admittedly, a small measure of speculation is involved. Nevertheless, I believe my interpretation is, on the whole, accurate.

"When Ahmad returned home after his release by Vartan, he intended to keep his promise. He commanded a chess set to be made. He entrusted delivery of this gift to a loyal retainer and provided him with an armed escort to conduct him to Vartan's realm. Ahmad's gift, however, never came into Vartan's hands.

"As I interpret certain of the documents, Ahmad's vizier was dismayed at his king offering such a gift to an enemy —the chess set was immensely valuable. The vizier schemed to acquire it for himself.

"Accordingly, he hired a band of robbers to attack the emissary, seize the chess pieces, and secretly bring them back to him. Since the attack would take place in Vartan's territory, King Ahmad would blame Vartan's warriors.

"The vizier's plan failed to this extent: The chess set was never returned to him. Indeed, it vanished entirely. I am convinced it existed, but its whereabouts have remained unknown.

"The facts, my dear Miss Holly, are perhaps not as entertaining as the fiction. They have only the advantage of being true."

"Hold on a minute," said Vesper, instead of thanking Dr. Helvitius for his lucid exposition. "What evidence are you talking about? At first, you'd said there wasn't any. When I searched the archives, all the documents from that time were missing. Did they suddenly turn up again? That's magical."

Dr. Helvitius smiled indulgently. "We scholars have other techniques. Ah—collateral corroboration, evidentiary implications . . . I shall not bore you with details."

"I'm not bored," said Vesper. "I'd like to know more. I'd also like to know what you'd have done if you hadn't found us."

"I was prepared to conduct my own exploration—on your behalf, naturally. In the spirit of academic fellowship and collegiality, I would have shared my discoveries with you.

"You see, Miss Holly, I have concluded that the attack on Ahmad's emissary took place in this area. I, too, have a theory: Set upon by assassins, Ahmad's people might have escaped, fled, and sought refuge in the very structure we see before us. In those days, it would not have been in its present state of ruination."

What a pleasure it was to observe the workings of the scholar's intellect. It inspired me to offer some elaborations of my own. I suggested that when Ahmad's retainers found refuge in the temple, the assassins pursued them into the underground chambers. There, the emissary and his men made a last stand, protecting the gift to Vartan.

"Why, then," asked Helvitius, "did the assassins not make off with their prize?"

"That is a question whose answer has been lost in the mists of time," I replied. "The fact remains: The chessmen exist. We, sir, have discovered them."

Vesper must have grown excited by my remarks, for her foot kept twitching against my shin.

Helvitius leaned forward. "The actual chessmen? I congratulate you. May I assume you will extend to me the same professional courtesy I would have extended to you? If you would permit me to examine this long-lost treasure—"

"There are many other treasures as well. Greater than anyone suspected," I said. "Yes, of course, we welcome your examination and the benefit of your opinion."

"Not now." Vesper turned hastily to me. "We can't stay here any longer."

I had completely forgotten, my thoughts distracted by the scholar's brilliant exposition. We had promised Nilo the safety of traveling with us. He was, in fact, making discreet but urgent gestures.

"Miss Holly, you astonish me," said Helvitius. "Having reached your goal, do you propose to abandon it?"

"We have something else to do first," said Vesper. "I'm not abandoning anything."

"Naturally, you will not object to my pursuing my own investigations during your absence?"

"I do object," said Vesper. "Any investigations to be done—we'll be the ones to do them."

"Miss Holly, my equipment is excellent," replied Helvitius. "Need I point out that you have none at all?"

He was, as he said, completely outfitted. His supplies even included a case of dynamite. Surely, I remarked, he did not contemplate using high explosive that might further damage the structure.

"It is my own formulation," Dr. Helvitius answered. "An improvement on the invention of Herr Nobel. Have no fear, professor. As a chemist as well as an experienced mining engineer, I am accustomed to dealing with volatile substances."

"No one's going to deal with anything until we get back," said Vesper. "Right now, I only want the chessmen. They're the evidence we need. We'll take them with us. I'm going to the chamber to collect them."

Beckoning to Nilo, she started up the slope. I followed, as did Helvitius, who continued his attempt at persuading Vesper to change her mind.

"Allow me, at least, to assist you," he said when he saw the rope we had used as a means of entry. Several of his crew had trailed after him; he instructed one to fetch some items from the pack. The Zentan soon hurried back with a rope ladder and several excellent lanterns.

Nilo had already clambered down. Vesper paused for a moment. "This gear looks familiar," she muttered to me. "In fact, it looks like ours."

They were, I assured her, standard items commonly available. We discussed it no further, as Nilo was calling for us to make haste. Dr. Helvitius climbed after me. Once we reached what I chose to call the sanctum, I directed his attention to the row of ancient figures.

Surprisingly, he showed no interest. Instead, he pulled away brusquely and went into the anteroom, where Vesper and Nilo were busily picking up the scattered chessmen.

I stood a moment, admiring once again the array of priceless statuary. In that instant, all grew clear to me. How had I failed to realize it? How had Vesper, with her keen mind, overlooked an obvious explanation? I hurried to the anteroom.

"That reprehensible *bimbashi*!" I cried. "Dear girl, do you wonder he did all in his power to hinder us? He wanted the statues for himself. He feared we would discover those marvelous figures before he could remove them."

How easy it would be, I went on, for Zalik to sell the valuable artifacts, no questions asked, to collectors, dealers, and sad to say, respectable museum curators.

"I doubt that," said Vesper. "He might not have known about the temple. If he did know, he could have cleared it out whenever he wanted. Nothing kept him from coming up here and ransacking the place.

"No—there is something that might have stopped him," Vesper went on, pondering her own words. "He might have been told to keep away. Ordered to keep hi nose out of the whole business."

That, I replied, was most unlikely. As regional comman der, Zalik would follow no one's orders but his own.

"No, professor," put in Helvitius. "Miss Holly is cor rect. "The diligent colonel has his instructions."

"Who from?" Vesper rounded on Helvitius. "Do yo know?"

"I do," Helvitius replied. "The *bimbashi*, in fact, serve two masters. One is Ergon Pasha."

"And the other?" asked Vesper.

Dr. Helvitius smiled. "Myself."

# 14

I have always considered myself a keen judge of character and have taken a measure of pride in my ability to perceive an individual's true nature on short acquaintance. Granted, I was wrong in the case of Nilo, Milan, Silvia, Matrona Mira, and Colonel Zalik—but under the circumstances, my mistakes were justifiable. In my estimation of Dr. Helvitius, my error was profound and unforgivable. Still, one is always reluctant to think ill of a colleague.

Even as he spoke, I could not believe my ears. Perhaps his studies had overtaxed his brain and he had gone a little mad. Dr. Helvitius, however, gave no sign of mental derangement. He remained cool and matter-of-fact, though his words implied his possible involvement in a highly unethical enterprise.

Nilo, sensing treachery and danger, started forward, at the same time reaching into his jacket. The two Zentans, having followed their employer, prevented Nilo from defending us by pointing rifles at him.

Dr. Helvitius took possession of the pistol which Nilo had been unable to draw, retained the weapon, and aimed it at us. His attitude was unmistakably threatening.

Vesper—my admiration for the dear girl's calm courage leaped to still greater heights—gave no sign of panic or dismay. Hands on hips, she stood and leveled her glance on Helvitius.

"I can't say you surprised me," declared Vesper. "I always thought you took those documents from the archives, but I never imagined you'd come chasing after us."

"I sincerely wish I had not been obliged to," said Helvitius.

"So do I," said Vesper. "Why did you?"

"When Colonel Zalik notified us that you were beyond his observation and control," replied Helvitius, "I felt that I must take a personal hand in the matter.

"Believe me, Miss Holly, I regret this unhappy outcome. Had you been kept from journeying into this region, I would have been spared the need for such direct action. Alas, the man who accosted you in the Old Town proved inefficient."

"Oh?" said Vesper, not in reproach or anger but in a tone of welcome enlightenment. "You and Ergon Pasha were the ones who tried to have me killed?"

"Not exactly," said Helvitius. "Only to a degree."

"What's a degree of being dead?" returned Vesper.

"I mean that our purpose was not to kill you," said Helvitius. "You were only to be incapacitated, prevented from pursuing your investigations, thus allowing me to pursue my own without interference.

"No, Miss Holly, we did not wish your death. Not then. Now, it may be an unfortunate necessity for all of you."

"Do I understand you, sir?" I burst out. "You contemplate murdering us?"

"I must do more than contemplate it," said Helvitius.

My heart sank. Zalik was not the one who wished to plunder the ruins, but Helvitius himself and Osman's own vizier. How greed corrupts even those of high station! Yet I did not abandon hope. I had only one resource to dissuade him.

I appealed to his better nature.

I addressed him not as a gentleman and a scholar, but at least as a gentleman, which I hoped he was. A scholar, clearly, he was not.

"Sir, you do me an injustice," Helvitius replied. "Scholarship and research rank high among my many interests. Some of your most distinguished journals have published my papers—not, of course, under my true name—in the realms of chemistry, physics, and biology. My contributions have not gone unrecognized."

The villain was actually proud of himself! I employed a most severe tone, sparing him nothing of my shock and disapproval.

"Dr. Helvitius," I said, "you claim to be a man of intellect and learning. Your behavior, nevertheless, has shown otherwise. You have lost my respect. You, sir, are no better than a common thief."

"No, Brinnie," put in Vesper. "He's a very uncommon one."

"Professor Garrett," said Helvitius, "you have assumed I seek those ancient figures. You are wrong. I recognize their value, but they hold no interest for me. I desire only one object, and that object I am resolved to possess."

He turned and directed his remarks to Vesper. "I require the chessmen which, regrettably, you discovered before I did. More precisely, I require one of them: the piece wrought in the form of King Ahmad."

"We don't have it," said Vesper. "You can see for yourself. If we did have it, I certainly wouldn't give it to you."

"Miss Holly, I remind you that your life hangs by a thread. I advise you to comply with my demand, unless you wish that thread to be snapped."

"You'll do that anyway," retorted Vesper, "whether we give you the chessman or not. You won't dare let us go now. Brinnie and I are a danger to you. There's no use promising to keep our mouths shut. You can't trust us any more than we can trust you. You'll have to get rid of us.

"But our *dragoman* has no part in this, he doesn't give a hoot about your schemes, whatever they are. You have no reason to harm him. Let him go."

"*Lincilla,*" Nilo broke in, "as I told you, I do not beg or plead, even for my life, nor will I allow you to do so for me."

"I do not wish to seem uncompassionate, Miss Holly," replied Helvitius, "but the stakes are too high to allow me that luxury."

"So, you'll kill us all," said Vesper. "Then what? You still won't have the chess king."

"I shall find it," said Helvitius, "if I must upturn and sift through every stone."

"Suppose it isn't here."

"Then," said Helvitius, "I shall comb this area inch by inch, a task which will be facilitated by your permanent absence. Do not underestimate my determination. The prize is worth every effort."

"A chessman can't be that valuable," said Vesper, "not even one made of solid gold covered with diamonds."

"Which it is not," replied Helvitius. "Its intrinsic worth is slight. As an essential aspect of my plan, it is beyond price as the magnitude of my endeavor is beyond even your comprehension. The scale is large, Miss Holly. It encompasses the very future of Illyria.

"I refer to natural resources," Helvitius continued. "Thousands of acres of woodland for timber. Mineral wealth. The construction of railways. Ergon Pasha has agreed—for a share in the profits, naturally—that I shall be granted *firmans,* licenses, concessions, in all these enterprises.

"When rebellion and unrest are stamped out once and for all, I shall begin my projects in a peaceable atmosphere, unhindered by troublemakers and malcontents."

"That isn't beyond my comprehension," said Vesper. "I comprehend it very well. It's robbery. Large-scale, as you say. But robbery no matter how you look at it. I'm afraid you're going to be disappointed."

"I doubt that, Miss Holly."

"I don't," said Vesper. "You've forgotten one thing. Ergon Pasha doesn't have the last word in handing out concessions and trade licenses. Osman does."

"I am aware of it."

"Then you ought to be aware that he'll never agree. He told me so himself. Osman will never turn Illyria over to foreign interests. He knows they'd milk the country dry. You've been wasting your time."

"I think not," said Helvitius. "You, Miss Holly, assume that King Osman will continue to occupy the throne."

These words astonished even Vesper. She stood silent a long moment.

"Of course. That's it," she said at last. "It's logical. You'll have to kill Osman, too."

"Say, rather, a reorganization of government," replied Helvitius. "When the time is ripe, King Osman will be eliminated and replaced by a more compliant monarch. One who appreciates our efforts and will graciously accept a share in the benefits. Simple statecraft, Miss Holly. It has happened elsewhere and often."

"You'll never manage it," returned Vesper. "I'm sure Osman's very well guarded."

"Guarded from all but those closest to his person and least suspected. His barber, Miss Holly, and his tailor.

"It has already been arranged. Those two have been handsomely paid to serve us. Further, when their task is done, they have been instructed to leave unmistakable indications that the heinous crime was perpetrated by Illyrian ethnics."

Nilo, at this, broke into a number of comments regarding Zentan perfidy. Helvitius, though, had been correct. Conspiracies of this sort are far from unknown in history. However, that a gentleman, let alone a king, might not be safe in the hands of his own tailor and barber—this was monstrous past belief.

"Your knowledge of our plan, Miss Holly, now enhances the need to dispose of you," said Helvitius. "As you would be the first to recognize, we have no choice."

"Murderous villain!" I cried. "You mean to shoot us down in cold blood!"

"Indeed not," Helvitius calmly replied. "You shall remain here. It would be unwise if you vanished entirely. It would lead to a search that might prove inconvenient to me and raise embarrassing questions if your bodies were discovered with signs of deliberate violence. I shall arrange a fate more plausible and less suspicious.

"Ancient structures are notoriously unreliable. This temple has already suffered damage. What could be more natural than for all of you to perish in a further collapse of these chambers? I should then conduct an excavation in the forlorn hope of finding you alive. A hope, of course, which will not be fulfilled."

Helvitius turned on his heel and made his way to the rope ladder and, with great agility, climbed up.

The Zentans also withdrew, still training their rifles on us. Moments later, the ladder itself was hauled upward.

"Dear child," I cried, "we must escape from this place!"

"No question about that, Brinnie," said Vesper. "If there's another way out, we'd better find it." She hesitated. "I still don't see what the chess king has to do with this. I should have asked Helvitius when I had the chance."

Vesper and Nilo cast about for any unsuspected egress. I went hastily to examine the farther end of the passage, hoping there might be a fissure in the walls, a branching tunnel, or anything that might lead us to safety. I found nothing. Even if I had, the vile Helvitius and his crew were still above us.

"Brinnie, get away from there!"

Vesper and Nilo were racing toward me. I glanced back to see the object of their concern.

Though I recognize and applaud the benefits of Herr Alfred Nobel's invention applied to mining operations, dam building, and other types of useful construction, at that moment I wished the illustrious Swede had never set foot in a laboratory.

With sputtering fuse attached, a bundle of dynamite had come hurtling down the shaft.

# ❧ 15 ❧

"Brinnie, get back! Move!" cried Vesper as I stood rooted to the spot, appalled by the method Helvitius had adopted for our destruction. Killing us was, in itself, criminal in the extreme; to do so with deliberate disregard for a noble monument to antiquity was nothing less than heartless vandalism. The fuse, meantime crackling and sparking, grew alarmingly shorter every second.

Nilo would have thrown himself on this infernal device in an attempt to snuff out the fuse or to shield us with his own person. Realizing his gallant but lunatic intention, Vesper seized him, spun him around, and sent us all stumbling through the first available portal—the entry to the sanctum.

There, we flung ourselves to the ground, covered our heads with our arms as the shock of the blast jolted into the chamber. The ceiling shuddered, a supporting beam groaned and cracked, showering dirt and gravel upon us. Ancient dust filled the air. Blessedly, one of our lanterns had been left in the sanctum, though its light offered only a glimmer in the reeking cloud.

I staggered, coughing, to my feet. Vesper and Nilo had picked themselves up, neither of them hurt; all of us, though, were equally stunned and deafened.

As my head ceased reeling and my thoughts grew more coherent, I hurriedly proposed what seemed our only course of action. We had not explored beyond our immediate vicinity. Other chambers doubtless lay farther down the passageway. What they might give in the way of protection, I could not guess. In any event, we would be no worse off than we already were.

Vesper snatched up the lantern. Instead of following me to the doorway, she turned back toward the rank of statues, which had remained upright in spite of the blast.

I pleaded for her to join us. This was not the moment to think of salvaging old Illyrian artifacts, no matter what their value. Helvitius, beyond a doubt, would bombard us again and continue doing so until satisfied he had reduced us, and the temple, to rubble. The villain even now was probably setting new explosive charges.

"He wants the chess king," Vesper called over her shoulder. "If it's so important, we mustn't let him have it."

"*Lincilla,* this no longer matters," insisted Nilo. "We have no time to search. Whether you find it or not, none of us may escape with our lives."

Vesper's optimism astonished me. The dear child simply refused to consider the likelihood of this chamber becoming, at any instant, our tomb.

"The village dancers," Vesper said, "the months, the seasons changing in the pattern of their dance. They were a human calendar."

I broke in impatiently to reply that I quite understood it; the ritual was found in many cultures, and a discussion of comparative mythologies now would cost us precious time. Finding an air shaft, even an animal's burrow, might be our only hope.

"These figures," Vesper went on. "Something about them jangled me. I couldn't put my finger on it until I saw them again. I knew they were January, February, and all the rest. Helvitius never noticed. He was too busy looking for the chess king.

"Don't you see, Brinnie?" Vesper said, as if that obscure Illyrian ceremony were crystal clear to any observer and the statuary itself held the key to the ancient riddle.

I admitted I had no idea what she meant.

"The thirteenth month."

Vesper scrambled onto the ledge, picked up a figure, and sprang back to the ground.

"Thirteen, Brinnie, instead of twelve." She held up a statue some dozen inches tall, like the others. "When the Zentans were attacked, I'd guess that one of them must have hidden the piece where nobody would think of looking—with all the other statues. Who'd notice one among a crowd?"

The object which Vesper showed me was a Zentan king in full royal regalia. Though I could not attest that it bore any actual likeness to King Ahmad, I had no doubts whatever: This was the prize Helvitius sought. It had been under his very nose, in plain sight; he had fallen victim to his own mental nearsightedness. Cold comfort, given our present situation.

Vesper's explanation was not the calm, reflective discourse it may have seemed from the foregoing account.

Nilo kept breaking in impatiently, tugging at Vesper's arm, urging her to lose no more time. Finally, he resorted to taking hold of her and hauling her almost bodily to the sanctum doorway.

He could not have chosen a worse moment. Helvitius touched off another explosive charge. The beams and pillars framing the portal broke and toppled. The blast threw me backward. Regaining my feet, I stared horror-stricken. Vesper and Nilo had disappeared beneath the rubble.

I can give no clear description of my actions immediately following this catastrophe. My thoughts were only of Vesper. I was dimly aware, then, of flinging myself on the debris, scrabbling at the loose stones, casting aside shattered fragments.

Where and how I found strength for a task that would have daunted me in other circumstances, I do not know. Shouting Vesper's name, I plunged bare-handed against what appeared a pile of giant jackstraws, bending every effort yet, at the same time, fearful that my work would result in further collapse of the surrounding structure.

Heaving away one jagged stone, I saw Vesper's face, begrimed and dust-streaked, grinning broadly at me. Her marmalade hair was sprinkled with dirt and gravel.

"Be careful, Brinnie. Nilo's right behind me. There's a beam or something holding up the pile. Don't jar it loose, it's keeping us from being squashed."

With a cry of joyous relief, I fell to work again, this time more cautiously. Vesper soon gained enough freedom of movement to help me from her side. At last, she was able to crawl out and we both concentrated our full attention on extricating Nilo.

His face was bruised and scraped, but he assured us he

had suffered no irreparable damage. He did, however, show some astonishment at the pile of rubble I had so frantically cleared away.

"You don't know Brinnie," Vesper said. "When it comes right down to it, he's still a tiger."

The dear child flung her arms around me in a gritty embrace, then returned to the pile of rubble and hauled out the Zentan chessman. To me, this object was the least of our concerns. We still had our lives, but were worse off than ever, being blockaded and trapped within the sanctum. We had, momentarily, escaped being crushed, only to face the final ordeal of suffocation. I turned once more to the labor of clearing a passage, cursing Helvitius with every breath —which I could ill afford to waste.

Nilo joined me. I expected Vesper to aid us by applying her natural vitality to our desperate efforts. Perhaps she had already calculated the work to be futile, for she was standing staring at the far side of the chamber. The ledge had broken in two, tumbling the ancient statuary to the ground. The figures themselves had not been damaged. Were I of a fanciful turn of mind, I would have said their expressions of antique calm reflected assurance they would endure long after we mortals had perished miserably.

What puzzled me, however, was why our lantern still burned and gave such strong illumination.

Only then, as Vesper beckoned to us, did I understand. What I took for lantern light was a clear and golden ray of sun. The ceiling above the ledge had collapsed—but had fallen so as to leave a gap to the surface. Vesper clambered up the mound of rubble and began clawing away at the opening, striving to enlarge it. Nilo and I abandoned our fruitless digging to help her.

Sublime irony! Helvitius, attempting to destroy us, had provided our means of liberation. Vesper's words dampened my newly risen spirits.

"Not so fast, Brinnie," she warned. "We can't go jumping out like a jack-in-the-box. We don't dare make this hole much bigger, either. Helvitius and his gang are still up there. They'll spot us as soon as we climb above ground."

We were, in fact, no better off than we had been. Sooner or later, Helvitius would explode more charges. Once he decided we had been sufficiently pulverized or suffocated, he and his men would dig their way into the chamber. If not our lifeless bodies, he would find us clinging here like bats, or pitiful prisoners staring from a peephole in their dungeon.

On top of that, Vesper had done him the service of finding the chess king. He need only take it from her hands. As for us, he would merely devise another method of destruction—hardly a problem for one of his fiendish ingenuity.

Vesper, meantime, ventured to crawl up and, with extreme caution, peer out the opening. No sooner had she lifted her head the slightest fraction than rifle fire burst above us.

## ❧ 16 ❧

Vesper withdrew her head instantly. But the dear girl's eternal curiosity was such that, before Nilo and I could prevent her, she peered out again.

"Nobody's shooting at *us,*" Vesper exclaimed. "There's a—well, it looks like a band of gypsies. They're firing at Helvitius and the Zentans."

The shock of the explosions and the strain of her ordeal had, I feared, deranged the poor child's perception. Gypsies roaming the Silvana Forest? Those peaceful horse traders and fortune-tellers would have found few customers in these uplands.

Nilo took Vesper's place at the opening, then began scrabbling at the rubble. "*Lincilla,* help me."

Handing me the chess piece, Vesper lent all her efforts to enlarging the gap. She and Nilo had both lost their wits, in my estimation. Helvitius already posed a sufficient threat without letting ourselves be caught up in the midst of rampaging readers of tea leaves. Nilo, by this time, had scrambled free, pulling Vesper with him.

"Come on, Brinnie," Vesper cried. "Out you go."

I had no real choice, since she and Nilo had seized hold of me and were hauling me upward despite my protest that I had been snagged on a broken stone as firmly as if in the grim clutch of Helvitius himself. Finally, they heaved me loose, though I was obliged to leave behind a portion of my garments and a few shreds of skin.

Vesper retrieved the chessman from me and tucked it under her arm. Nilo shouted at us to hurry, urging us down the slope. I had only a momentary glance, enough to see that Vesper had not been mistaken. Some figures in colorful gypsy garb were directing a brisk fusillade against the vile doctor and his hirelings, forcing them to take cover behind fallen pillars. I recognized one man with a bright cloth tied around his head—Milan.

Whatever unfriendly thoughts I once harbored were forgotten. I cheered at the welcome sight of him. The stouthearted Milan had no doubt grown alarmed at our lengthy absence and had come seeking us. He and his companions obviously had chosen gypsy apparel as a disguise during their prospective journey.

While Milan and his fellows held off the Zentans, I went half tumbling to the bottom of the slope. Nilo was already there, well in command, ordering Silvia and another of his followers to untether the Zentan pack animals, to seize whatever supplies could easily be carried, and to wreak havoc in the camp. He was good at his work, very competent and businesslike, more so than when he had been our *dragoman*.

By now, our rescuers began withdrawing from the temple site, all the while keeping the Zentans at a safe distance from us. Nilo gestured for Vesper and me to climb astride the mules. Nilo took the horse of Dr. Helvitius, and we set off with all possible speed. Milan and his companions acted as rear guard, joining us when we had outdistanced any pursuers.

Only once did Nilo permit us to halt and rest, while he, Milan, and Silvia conferred briefly. From their conversation, I gathered that a wagon had been obtained and hidden near Alba-Collia, ready for our use.

Vesper propped herself against a tree, taking advantage of these moments to examine the chess piece, that object which had nearly cost our lives.

"It's beautifully made," Vesper said, turning the figure around and around in her hands, "but Helvitius was right when he told us it wasn't all that valuable. No fabulous gems set in it, no gold or silver."

Hardly a spectacular gift from one king to another, I observed. I suggested burying it. Vesper had achieved her goal of keeping it from the villainous doctor, and I saw no point in adding to our burdens.

"Bury it?" returned Vesper. "After all we went through? No, we'll hang on to it. I'll have to figure out why Helvitius and Ergon Pasha want it so badly."

She continued studying the figure. "Something's inscribed here, around the pedestal." Vesper rubbed the base of the chessman with a corner of her sleeve. "Can you make it out?"

I shook my head. The light was fading, the letters had been tarnished by the centuries, and Nilo, furthermore, was goading us to get a move on.

"I'll see that later," Vesper said. "The most important

thing right now is to warn Osman. They mean to kill him —but when? Helvitius didn't tell us. I only hope we won't be too late. I'll ask Nilo what he can do to help."

She did not have the opportunity just then, Nilo being occupied with getting our party in order and on the way again. We continued through the woods, despite the deepening shadows. Night fell, but we pressed on. Nilo, I had to recognize, was every bit as redoubtable as the original Vartan must have been. He seemed to know every twist and turn of every trail; there were times when I could have sworn the fellow was able to see in the dark. He set such a vigorous pace, even his own people showed signs of flagging. I had already run out of wind miles before. Vesper, needless to say, kept up with him. With the pair of them cajoling us, or sometimes browbeating us, egging us on, adding the occasional old Illyrian proverb, we came out of the forest a little before daybreak, exactly as he had calculated.

I had hoped, then, that we could find our wagon and leave Alba-Collia well behind us. Nilo, however, led us to Matrona Mira's cottage, where more of his followers would meet us.

The spry old woman was expecting us. She hurried us indoors, fed us, bustled around pulling out sacks of provisions for our journey, as if she had done this sort of thing a dozen times—as she probably had.

The *matrona* was delighted to see Vesper, who showed her the chess piece and described briefly what we had found in Vartan's Castle.

"Someday there may be another legend," the old woman said, "of a girl who came from a faraway land and brought ancient treasure from the depths of the earth. Yes, child, I believe this is truly Ahmad's gift to Vartan. A curious gift. There is nothing in our lore to explain its meaning."

Vesper, however, was less concerned with the chess piece than with warning Osman about the threat to his life, and she took up this matter with Nilo.

"We don't dare lose time," Vesper told him. "Helvitius isn't going to sit on his hands. Will he try to follow us? Or get word to Ergon Pasha? There's no outguessing him. All I can see is for us to reach Osman as fast as we can."

"If you will do that, *Lincilla*," Nilo replied, "we must change our plan. My destination is off your road. If you travel with me, it will cost you three days' added journey."

"We have to stay together," Vesper said. "It's the safest way for you."

"Perhaps," answered Nilo. "But, *Lincilla*, you cannot follow both roads. If you would go straight to Zenta, we shall take leave of each other now. For me, the danger will be no greater than it has ever been. For yourself, you will have no difficulty. If you are stopped and questioned, you need only show Osman's letter and *firman*."

"Thank heaven for those," Vesper said. "We'd be lost without them."

The documents, I assured her, were carefully packed in my saddlebags. Even as I spoke, my mouth went suddenly dry.

"Dear girl—" I could barely whisper. "The documents indeed are in my saddlebags. The saddlebags are with our horses—"

I clutched my head. There was no need to say more. Vesper grasped the distressing truth.

"With our horses," she said, "and we left our horses at the temple."

Nilo stared at me, as appalled as I was.

"So much for the documents, then." Vesper bit her lips. After a few moments of hard thought, she glanced up at Nilo and me.

"No use crying over spilled milk or lost papers," Vesper said. "They're gone. That's a fact. We have to deal with it. Only it does turn things around. We were going to help Nilo. Now he can help us.

"Without our papers, we can't risk being stopped. Nilo, do you know a way of getting us to Zenta? Can your people pass us along from one place to the next? Secretly—and fast?"

"To save the life of a Zentan king?" Nilo's face darkened. "*Lincilla,* ask anything but that."

"It would help your own cause," Vesper insisted. "I'll tell Osman you kept him from being assassinated. He'll be grateful."

"Gratitude from a Zentan?" retorted Nilo.

"Ahmad was grateful to Vartan."

"And gave him a chess game. *Lincilla,* my people demand more than that."

Nilo turned away. Vesper was not going to let matters rest there. Before she could marshal her powers of persuasion, Silvia burst into the cottage.

She had gone to fetch our wagon. What she brought was disaster.

"Zentan cavalry! In the village!" cried Silvia. "They seek the two *farenkis.*"

I sprang to my feet. In that instant, I knew what must be

done. The *matrona*'s legend set me the example. "The wolves!" I cried. "The Zentan prince led them astray!

"Save yourself, dear girl, for we must no longer think of saving Osman. Stay with Nilo. Go wherever he wishes. Only leave here immediately.

"These creatures of Helvitius and Ergon Pasha mean to arrest us—and so they shall. Not you, dear child. Myself. Let them try to capture me while you make your escape. If I can elude them, I shall find you later. If I cannot, then I pray that we shall meet in a happier place."

"Brinnie," said Vesper, "that's the most ridiculous thing I've ever heard."

Disregarding her words, without hesitation or a backward glance, I ran from the cottage and leaped astride one of the horses. Vesper called after me; I turned a deaf ear to her entreaties and galloped for Alba-Collia.

# ❧ 17 ❧

Of the incident that followed, the less said the better. If modesty forbids boasting of one's accomplishments, surely a similar veil of decency may be drawn over one's mistakes.

In short, inspired by the legend, my plan succeeded. It succeeded all too well.

I did indeed gallop into the village, where half a dozen cavalrymen were halted in front of the *kaffenion*. I shouted that I was the individual they sought and, to incite them further, made a defiant and somewhat vulgar Illyrian gesture. I streaked past; the troopers wheeled and spurred after me.

As a decoy, my goal was to lead them as far afield for as long as possible. I bolted across the countryside, over ditches, and through farmyards, scattering chickens, leaving the peasantry gaping after me and the Zentans on my heels. How long this mad gallop lasted, I could not estimate. I was only aware that we covered some good distance. My horse would have gone many miles longer. Alas, we parted company at a high hedge.

I scrambled free of the tangled branches. The Zentans, a few yards behind, reined up and dismounted. Trapped with the hedge at my back, I adopted a pugilistic stance, resolving to sell my life dearly and to make that process a lengthy one. I defied them and their treacherous masters, Helvitius and Ergon Pasha. My death would gain them nothing.

"Your death?" replied the Zentan officer confronting me. "Sir, we desire only your safety. We have ridden here from the capital, by order of King Osman. His Majesty is gravely concerned for you and Miss Holly. He will soon order a punitive expedition against the rebels. He does not wish you to be caught up in the fighting. He sent us to find and bring you to him."

My dismay requires no description. Not only had I piled blunder on top of blunder, but also I realized that if they found Vesper, they would find her in the company of the very man Osman meant to destroy. Vesper would never forgive me for leading them to Nilo, nor would I forgive myself.

"Sir," I said. "I shall find Miss Holly. You and your men must return immediately and warn King Osman. His life is in danger. A foul conspiracy! The vizier! The barber! The tailor!"

At first, the Zentan stared as if my words were only the babbling of a demented *farenki*. The intensity of my emotion, however, carried conviction. The officer stood thoughtfully for some long moments.

"Sir," he said at last, "these are serious charges. They go beyond my responsibility and competence. You yourself must bring these accusations. I shall detail two of my men to continue searching for Miss Holly. You, sir, shall return with me to Zenta."

I protested in vain. The officer obliged me to mount. He issued his orders. We headed back toward the capital.

During the long days of the journey, I sought every opportunity to escape, but the Zentans did not let me out of their sight for a moment. I could only wonder, in anguish, if I would ever see the dear child again and how I could explain to Mary that Vesper might spend the rest of her life in the Illyrian backlands, surrounded by desperate rebels, never to set foot in Philadelphia again.

They delivered me at last, bedraggled and travel-stained, to the palace. It was well past midnight. The officer was relieved and delighted to get me off his hands and into those of a royal chamberlain. He spoke apart briefly with this functionary, who conducted me to an antechamber.

I demanded to see King Osman immediately. The gold-braided lackey pompously informed me that His Majesty was asleep, an audience now was impossible.

"Wake him up!" I exclaimed. "This is a matter of life or death—His Majesty's life or death!"

My words carried force enough to send him scurrying off, leaving me to cool my heels if not my impatience. The Zentan formalities for rousing a monarch in the middle of the night, whatever the emergency, seemed endless. I was beside myself when the door finally opened.

I jumped to my feet. "Your Majesty—"

The words died on my lips at the sight of Ergon Pasha.

The vizier strode toward me. "Professor Garrett, my pleasure is surpassed only by my surprise."

I was not inclined to exchange courtesies.

"You villain," I retorted, "we know your foul scheme. You and the unspeakable Helvitius."

"I fear the difficulties of your journey have done you serious harm," he answered. "I was informed that you brought a warning of an attempt on His Majesty's life. Your accusations are quite alarming."

He sadly shook his head. "I was shocked to hear them, and bewildered by such grave charges. Now I realize that you are distraught, not in possession of all your faculties."

"Scoundrel!" I flung at him. "You dare to call me mad?"

"Fevered," said Ergon Pasha. "An inflammation of the brain. You have, alas, fallen victim to a disease all too common in our northern region. You shall receive the best of medical attention."

"And you shall receive what you richly deserve. When the king learns I am here—"

"He will not," said Ergon Pasha. "The chamberlain very properly advised me first of your presence. I saw no reason to disturb His Majesty's repose. Affairs of state weigh so heavily on him.

"He will, in due course, be informed of your arrival and your unfortunate malady. By then, Professor Garrett, you will be in no condition to repeat your pitiful ravings. The ailment you suffer from is invariably fatal, but mercifully quick."

This new villainy left me aghast and speechless. Ergon Pasha withdrew. Moments later, half a dozen palace attendants arrived to surround and conduct me from the chamber.

I protested and struggled in vain. Vesper, at least, had

not fallen into this trap with me. Fortunately, she was many miles away.

"Brinnie, what are they doing to you?"

I could not believe my ears. Perhaps, indeed, I was feverish.

"Take your hands off him!"

Vesper had burst into the chamber and was already plunging into the midst of my captors, who were too astonished to do more than fall back out of her way. Behind her, I glimpsed Nilo.

"Come on. We have to see Osman."

"Dear girl," I cried, as she pulled me into the corridor. "Ergon Pasha knows—"

"I was afraid he'd got hold of you first. Nilo's people found out what happened after you dashed off. We tried to catch up with you. The palace guard's pretty upset; we didn't stand around to answer questions."

"You'll stir up a hornet's nest—"

"I hope so," replied Vesper.

If that had been her intention, she succeeded admirably. Osman's guards and attendants filled the corridor. At sight of Vesper, they raced toward her.

"Safety in numbers, Brinnie," said Vesper. "Ergon Pasha can't keep us quiet now."

Suiting her actions to her words, Vesper shouted at the top of her voice that Osman was in danger, demanding to be taken to him, and raising such a commotion that even the cooks and bakers must have heard it, let alone Ergon Pasha. I saw nothing of that reptile. No doubt he had made himself extremely scarce.

The crowd suddenly fell silent and drew back. Osman

himself had arrived. Still in his dressing gown, he glanced around bemused. Vesper ran up to him.

"Get yourself a new barber, Your Majesty," said Vesper, "and don't order any new clothes."

CHAPTER

## ❦ 18 ❦

"What about breakfast?" Vesper said, when she finished giving Osman an account of the conspiracy. She stretched out her legs on the divan in the royal apartment, where Osman had conducted us. The dear girl looked travel-worn, but unharmed and reasonably clean. I had never been happier to see anyone in my life.

"Your news has made me forget the obligations of hospitality." Osman, indeed, had been visibly shaken though he tried his best to cover it up. "A monarch should not be surprised by treachery. Nevertheless, Miss Holly, I owe you my life. You shall receive far more than a breakfast."

"Nilo's the one to thank," said Vesper. "He and his friends got us here in time."

"Against my will and against my better judgment." Until now, Nilo had been standing apart, arms folded, a dour expression on his face.

"But you did it, even so." Vesper turned to Osman.

"There's something else I have to tell you. Nilo isn't our *dragoman*. He used to be, for a while. But, as things turned out—"

"*Lincilla*," Nilo broke in, "let the Zentan king hear it from my own lips and know that I and my people defy him. I am Vartan."

Nilo, I thought, could have gone at it a little more tactfully. The king, after all, had barely recovered from his first shock. Osman sprang to his feet.

"How do you dare—" Osman's face had gone livid, his fists clenched. He rounded on Vesper. "Miss Holly, you know this is my sworn enemy. Yet, you bring him under my roof? You wish me to believe he had a part in saving my life? If he did, I reject it. I owe him nothing."

"You still owe me something," said Vesper. "You promised me a favor. I'll claim it now: Nilo's safety as long as he's with us."

"I made a promise and shall keep it," replied Osman. "Now I make another. Once he is out of your protection, he and his rebels shall have no mercy."

"We do not ask it," flung back Nilo, "nor shall we give it."

"You'll both be glad to change your minds," Vesper put in. "Nilo, you're forgetting that Osman doesn't know about the chess piece. When he does, he'll feel a lot differently."

"So you led me to believe, *Lincilla*," replied Nilo. "I doubted it then. I doubt it now."

Vesper unwrapped the bundle she had been carrying and held up the figure of Ahmad. "On the way here, I had a good look at it. The inscription's in Old Illyrian. Nilo and I managed to translate it: *I reach out my hand in peace.*

"Ahmad's gift never reached Vartan. I wish it had. The

inscription, by the way, means exactly what it says. I found that out too. Here, I'll show you. The arm's jointed.

"The piece isn't important," Vesper added. "Not by itself. It's made to hold something."

Vesper carefully raised the chess king's arm. The front portion of the figure swung open—with some difficulty, for the spring mechanism had been unused for centuries. As Vesper showed us, the piece was, in effect, a container.

It was empty.

I could not stifle a groan of dismay. We had been almost blown to bits, buried alive, chased over the countryside—for nothing.

"No," said Vesper. "For more than we could have guessed. Osman told me, the first time we met, he wished for something to let him make an honorable peace. Well, there was something. Helvitius and Ergon Pasha found out about it from the old archives. Helvitius knew it had to be destroyed. If it had come to light, Osman could have made terms with the Illyrians. They'd have supported him and helped him build up the country—as Osman always wanted. Helvitius and his concessions and trade licenses would have been out the window. Ahmad's gift really was a gift beyond price."

"Dear girl," I cried, "then where is it?"

"I gave it away," said Vesper. "I gave it to the one who was supposed to have it in the first place—Vartan. The newest Vartan, anyway. Go on, Nilo, let them see for themselves."

Nilo pulled a roll of parchment from his jacket and passed it to Vesper. "I trust only your hands to hold this."

"Osman won't tear it up," Vesper said. "Not when he

realizes that it's a message from Ahmad to Vartan. Better than a message. I'd call it an official state document.

"Without going through all the old-style language, what Ahmad says here is that he offers peace between Zentans and Illyrians and all their descendants. He declares that the country belongs to both alike. From now on, they will fight only on the chessboard, not the battlefield. Ahmad was a gallant king, so was Vartan. As they were in the *Illyriad.*"

"*Lincilla,*" said Nilo, "we are not dealing with heroes of legend. Those words were written generations ago."

"Then," said Vesper, "it's high time you both did something sensible about them. Nilo, you told me it was against your honor to beg. You said you wouldn't plead for what your people should have by right. You don't need to. That was settled long ago."

She turned to Osman. "You told me you'd give justice, but you wouldn't have it forced out of you. No one's forcing or threatening you now. I think you said something about following in the footsteps of King Ahmad. It seems to me he's made his footsteps very plain."

Vesper handed the parchment to Osman. He studied it, then passed it to me for my own examination. I scrutinized it and assured him there was no question in my mind: The document was genuine. I also tried to explain its exceptional value as a rare example of early Zentan calligraphy.

Osman appeared little interested in these details. He walked to his window and gazed out for some while, saying nothing.

"I warned you, *Lincilla,*" muttered Nilo. "He will not be bound by words on an ancient scrap of paper."

Osman turned back. "I am not Ahmad, nor are you

Vartan. Yet, as in our *Illyriad,* once again an Illyrian has spared the life of a Zentan. I revere my ancestor, and shall do as he did. I, too, reach out my hand."

Which, in fact, he did—to the astonishment of Nilo, who hesitated a good long moment before grasping it.

"Remember what I said in the cave, Brinnie?" remarked Vesper. "The two of them were pulling at opposite ends of the same rope? I think they've just quit doing that."

# ❊ 19 ❊

"The trouble with skyrockets is," observed Vesper, "after the first couple of hundred, it's hard to tell the difference. The same with state banquets."

Her comments were justified. Official ceremonies, even the best intended, grow tiresome beyond a certain point. Therefore, I shall not dwell in detail on events following Osman's proclamation of equality for all his subjects. It suffices to say that Vesper, Nilo, and I were obliged to attend an assortment of formal dinners—indigestible to everyone but Vesper—and an endless round of diplomatic receptions—tedious to everyone, especially Vesper.

She did enjoy the rejoicing in the streets by the ethnic Illyrians—and by most of the Zentans, for that matter. Crowds gathered whenever she appeared and cheered her as much as they did Nilo and Osman. The Zentan women insisted upon wearing pantaloons copied after her own. The admiration showered on her would have turned the head even of a Philadelphian, but the dear girl took it all in stride.

On our last ceremonial occasion, Osman awarded her the Illyrian Star of Honor, First Class. I received a kind of certificate of merit.

"It doesn't give you half enough credit," remarked Vesper, "but the lettering's nice."

We spent the summer excavating the temple and retrieved the statuary undamaged. Vesper carefully mapped the site for the benefit of future scholars and prepared an excellent sketch of the temple as she supposed it had been in its original state. (This information later appeared in the monograph she wrote and published along with proof of her father's theory.)

A prolonged search revealed no trace of Ergon Pasha or Colonel Zalik. They had, no doubt, betaken themselves to some obscure corner of the world. Helvitius, too, had vanished.

"I'd like it better if I knew where he was," Vesper said. "I'd rather keep an eye on him than him keep an eye on us. He's not the sort who'll forgive and forget."

Nilo came to Alba-Collia as often as he could, to observe our progress, though his own duties occupied much of his time. He had agreed to serve as the king's adviser as long as Osman required.

Vesper showed no sign of wanting to leave Illyria. Only when I insisted, reminding her we had much to do at home, did she reluctantly agree. We embarked late in September after a final audience with Osman.

"Take with you the gratitude of my people," he said, "and, Miss Holly, the affection of their king."

Osman, I noticed, appeared quite downcast at Vesper's departure. So did Nilo, even more so.

He came to see us off, and I expected him to trot out an old Illyrian proverb. He only grinned at me and said that if I ever needed a *dragoman,* he hoped I would keep him in mind. (I presumed he was merely indulging in Illyrian humor and did not intend his offer to be taken seriously.)

"*Graciva Lincilla,*" he said, putting his hands on Vesper's shoulder, "you have done more than Vartan himself. Think of him as he thinks of you."

"I won't forget Vartan," replied Vesper, "but I'll remember him better as Nilo."

Vesper embraced him and ran to her cabin. When I joined her, I observed that she was crying—the first time I had seen her give way to such behavior.

To cheer her up, I pointed out that she had saved a king's life, prevented a civil war, triumphed over her father's detractors, foiled an abominable villain, and contributed to scholarly knowledge. Only then did I suspect she had acquired a broken heart into the bargain.

Poor child, my own heart ached for her. While some maintain that such emotions in the young are no worse than a skinned knee, I believe they are as painful as they are to an adult. Vesper, nevertheless, was not given to moping. Except for an occasional watery look, she regained her usual spirits—by my reckoning, shortly after we left the Azores.

One further ordeal awaited us. The newspaper press had got wind of Vesper's exploits and a number of journalists met us when we docked. Vesper gave them a simple statement of the facts, but the press felt obliged to embroider it. One journal described her as "crowned with tresses of richly glowing amber; her alabaster features illumined with orbs of emerald hue, coruscating like twin jewels." Another depicted her as leading an army of Illyrian patriots, grappling hand to hand with a murderous hairdresser, and planting the Stars and Stripes on the summit of Mount Albor. (I was mentioned in passing, my name printed as "Burton Garter.")

In Philadelphia, happily reunited with my dear Mary, with Moggie the cat, my beehives, my unfinished history, and my work on Holly's papers, I prepared to settle into a life of tranquil industry.

Vesper's behavior of late has, however, given me cause for uneasiness. I cannot precisely lay my finger on it. She has been plunking her banjo as usual, rummaging in the library, delving into almanacs, and even scanning the newspapers. Harmless occupations individually, taken all together they convey a certain restlessness.

The dear girl, I fear, may be contemplating some alarming, disruptive, perhaps dangerous project. In which case, I would naturally do all in my power to keep her from any such rash or foolhardy enterprise. Unless she wished me to accompany her.